PILOT ERROR

By Bill Knox

PILOT ERROR

BILL KNOX

PUBLISHED FOR THE CRIME CLUB BY
DOUBLEDAY & COMPANY, INC.
GARDEN CITY, NEW YORK
1977

ISBN 0-385-12855-X
Library of Congress Catalog Card Number 76–50776
Copyright © 1977 by Bill Knox
All Rights Reserved
Printed in the United States of America
First Edition in the United States of America

For Gill

PILOT ERROR

CHAPTER ONE

It was 2 A.M. on Monday morning when the little aircraft fell out of the bright moonlight towards the sleeping city. Only one person saw it happen, an air traffic controller at Glasgow Airport, three miles away, and when the moving blip disappeared from his radar screen all he could do was press the red crash button. When a blip vanished that way it didn't come back.

The aircraft was a single-engined four-seater Beagle Pup with only twenty engine hours clocked up since its last C. of A. overhaul. It fell from fifteen hundred feet, slowly spinning all the way, moonlight glinting on its silver wings while the wind sang and buffeted the fuselage.

At the last moment the starboard wingtip clipped the parapet of a twenty-storey block of high-rise apartments. The outer four feet of wing tore away and stayed there, the rest of the aircraft cartwheeling madly.

Three seconds later the Beagle hit the ground and the tail assembly snapped off. The nose wheel and strut were thrown thirty feet and embedded in a parked car. The rest was a tearing rasp of tortured metal as the fuselage ploughed into a grass verge to end with its nose embedded in the soft soil.

Suddenly, briefly, there was silence again while lights began appearing on every floor of the apartment block till it shone like a startled beacon. Then a woman in curlers looked out of her window on the eighteenth storey and began screaming. She was still there and still screaming when a group of bewildered, sleepy-eyed tenants began emerging from the block with raincoats buttoned over their pyjamas.

One man had a torch. He reached the aircraft's cockpit, shone the beam into the twisted interior, then lurched across to the respectability of the gutter before he vomited.

Other tenants had stayed indoors but had reached for their telephones. A police car, an ambulance, a second police car and two fire engines arrived in that order within the next five minutes and their crews got to work.

The pilot was still alive when they got him out, but there wasn't much left of his face and the firemen had to use their emergency jacks to release his legs. The Beagle's engine block had pulped them and it had done even worse to his girl passenger. She was dead. At a guess, she had been young. Whether she had been pretty beforehand was academic.

One of the police patrol drivers helped carry the girl's body over to the grass verge. Then, almost reluctantly, he went back to the blood-spattered cockpit where something had caught his eye. Reaching in, he brought out an empty metal whisky flask and gave a long sigh.

He glanced back towards the dead girl. Someone had already covered her over with a dark plastic sheet. The police driver swore a soft, pitying benediction, then trudged back towards his car and its radio. As he reached for the microphone, the ambulance was already pulling away with the pilot aboard and a resuscitation unit aiding the faint pulse of life that still remained.

The police driver waited for a moment as the blue emergency lights flashed their way along the road. The odds were stacked against the pilot's still being alive by the time the ambulance reached a hospital.

For once, the police driver decided, he didn't give a damn.

Happy Monday, decided Detective Chief Inspector Colin Thane. He stood outside the main door of the big new red brick building which was Strathclyde Police Headquarters and gave an uncharacteristic scowl at the world. All around him the city of Glasgow looked almost clean and pleasant in the bright spring sunshine. But his throat was raw, his eyeballs felt as though they were made of sandpaper, and he wished he'd stayed in bed. He would be forty-two years of age in a few days' time and that didn't help either.

The Millside Division car that had brought him was heading round towards the parking lot. Across the street, a mongrel dog was lifting its leg at a lamppost and ignoring the traffic. Thane decided he was on the dog's side. The influenza virus sniping its way round Glasgow was medically a mild twenty-four-hour variety, but it was knocking hell out of most people while it had the chance.

Happy Monday. Thane squared his shoulders and entered the building. The cadet messengers in the lobby were talking about football and ignored the figure in a light-weight grey Lovat suit, but they ignored anyone who didn't belong to Headquarters.

From the lobby, Thane rode two floors up in an elevator with a trio of chattering typists, a civilian clerk and a computer technician who was whistling "Bye Bye Blackbird." He was glad when he left them and the elevator doors sighed shut again.

"God," said a cynical voice which made him turn his

head. "Did you see that bunch you came up with? It's getting to be so the last thing you find in Headquarters is a real live cop—sir."

He grinned at the elderly uniformed sergeant with a double row of medal ribbons on his tunic pocket, remembering the man as a veteran sergeant back in his own days as a youthful beat cop.

"What's your racket now, Charlie?" he queried.

The sergeant shrugged. "I thought I had made it. A nice, cushy number in Supply and Stores I could have spun out till pension time. But not any more—I'm foot-slogging for the Aliens Department. Scaring the hell out of wee foreigners who've let their visas run out."

Happy Monday, Thane thought again as the man ambled off. Plenty of cops, particularly the older men, were having to struggle to cope with change. Civilianisation, pulling cops out of office jobs that could be done by clerks or secretaries and putting the cops concerned back to real police work, was just one of them.

Everyone, in fact, was having problems large or small. It was all part of the fact that there was no longer such a thing as the City of Glasgow Police. They all belonged to a brand-new, monster-sized baby called Strathclyde Police.

Even Thane, ranking as the youngest divisional C.I.D. chief in the city, found some of it traumatic.

Colin Thane had the build of a man who had to be a cop—but the thinking kind of cop. Nudging six feet in height, burly to match but still only a couple of pounds over what had been his training weight when athletics had interested him, he had a cheerfully rugged face with keen brown eyes and a mouth which usually had a grin waiting at the corners.

His dark hair was a little longer than the police-preferred

style. Lately he'd kept forgetting to take time off to visit a barber—and anyway, his wife liked it that way. He also had two children, a mortgage with ten years still to run, and a rusting family car he shared with his wife on alternative days.

As a cop, his outlook was never totally predictable. He'd schooled himself to accept the rules, but if the end result seemed worth it, then he'd stretch these same rules to breaking point. His own squad at Millside Division would have added in chorus that when Thane backed a hunch he'd stay with it in a stubborn optimism which reduced everyone else around to a nervous frazzle.

Though things occasionally went wrong. At that moment a corner of his mind was wondering exactly what had happened this time—the summons from Headquarters, a curt telephone message, had come in just half an hour earlier as he'd reached Millside Division from home.

He shrugged, certain he'd find out quickly enough. When he cleared his throat experimentally again it was still raw, which didn't help. Gloomily, he set off down the carpeted corridor past a series of offices where every other door carried an assistant chief constable's name-plate.

There was a theory that the way assistant chiefs were increasing in number they had to be breeding somewhere. But it was one more sign of what was going on.

Scottish local government had gone through its first total reorganisation in centuries. All the old county and city hall structures had been wiped away and in their place Scotland had been chopped into a handful of vast new regional authorities. The same thing had happened to the old police structures, a series of shotgun weddings and integrations.

In theory Glasgow had been integrated into the vast Strathclyde region—a major slice of Scotland which took in half the nation's population, five previous police forces, and every kind of trouble from Saturday night back-street razor fights to cattle rustling. Out in the old counties, they put it differently, sometimes bitterly, that labels didn't matter and the city ruled.

Colin Thane stopped at the last door but one in the corridor, where the name-plate read ASSISTANT CHIEF CONSTABLE ILFORD. When he pressed the admission buzzer a green ENTER sign snapped back at him and he went in.

"Good morning, sir," he said hopefully to the bulkier of the two men seated in the room.

"It'll be even better when you've shut that damned door, Thane," said Ilford in a voice as hoarse as his own. "Want me to die of pneumonia, or were you born in a field?"

Thane closed the door and looked suitably sympathetic. As Chief Superintendent in charge of Glasgow's C.I.D., William "Buddha" Ilford had never been noted for sweetness and light. Promotion to archangel rank in the Strathclyde hierarchy had merely honed his general attitudes to life. A heavy-jowled man with thinning grey hair, he wore an old tweed suit which looked as though it had been knitted from barbed wire. Maybe it had been, to go with the image.

But the other man was a stranger, slim, much younger, smooth in a dark grey business suit but with a friendly, raw-boned face. His black leather briefcase, government issue, was lying on Ilford's desk and had already been opened. But somehow he didn't have the air or appearance of the average civil servant who came visiting.

"Right." Ilford dragged a handkerchief from a pocket, coughed into it in a way that purpled his face, then drew a deep breath to recover. "Thane, this is Captain Leslie, from the Department of Trade and Industry—"

"Accidents Investigations Branch," finished Leslie mildly. "I've come needing help."

"So sit down and listen, Thane." Buddha Ilford thumbed irritably towards a chair. "But stay clear of me. I've got the plague or worse—not that I'm expecting sympathy."

Thane decided his own croak wasn't going to rate. While Ilford began a grunting business of stuffing tobacco into the charred briar relic he called a pipe, he took the empty chair waiting beside Captain Leslie. He had a good idea now what it was about, and as soon as Ilford got his pipe going the C.I.D chief confirmed his guess.

"Captain Leslie's business is air crashes—formal government investigation and report," said Ilford heavily through his pipe smoke. "I'm presuming you know about the plane that came down on the edge of your patch last night."

Thane nodded. The Millside C.I.D. night desk sergeant had phoned him twice about it, the first time a stand-by call and the second, just after he'd got back to sleep again, to say he could go back to sleep again.

The Beagle had come down in Fortrose, a low-rental city housing development area which was one of Millside's problem territories. The particular apartment block it had clipped was home for a colony of persistent troublemakers —new detectives were sent out there to cut their teeth on some of its families and usually came back sadder and wiser.

"Were you out at the scene, Chief Inspector?" asked Captain Leslie, bridging the gap.

"No." Thane shook his head thankfully. "Uniformed branch handled it, start to finish. That's normal routine, unless you're talking about a disaster situation when everybody pitches in."

Ilford grunted agreement. "Read their report yet?"

"I haven't had time." Thane shivered and decided that once he'd got away he'd borrow a thermometer from somewhere.

What he did know was that two more of the Millside day-shift team were down with flu. He'd also seen the C.I.D. occurrence book—it held the usual overnight assortment of incident reports, from a whisky theft at the docks to a would-be rapist who had tried it on a young physical education teacher and now had a fractured skull.

"You'd better tell him, Leslie," croaked Ilford wearily. "We'll save time that way."

"I'll keep it as short as I can, I promise." Briskly, the department man reached into his briefcase. "You know the old adage—if you can't strike oil in five minutes, stop boring. Photographs first."

Thane took the bundle of pictures Leslie produced. The first was a library shot of a Beagle Pup, then the crash photographs began. They'd been taken by night, some with the outline of the high-rise block in the background, most of them for technical record rather than effect.

"You'll know we got the pilot out alive but that his female passenger was dead," said Leslie in a matter-of-fact voice. "From our viewpoint, of course, the actual accident investigation is made a lot easier by the fact that there was no fire after the crash—in this case, probably sheer luck. Anyway, we let the fire-service people decide they were quite happy first. Then we ran a basic survey of the aircraft. After that"—he paused and shrugged—"well, it was a complete departure from routine. But we acted on police advice and moved the wreckage by truck to Glasgow Airport, which certainly isn't normal procedure."

"There's nothing normal about anything that happens

out at Fortrose," said Ilford defensively. "Give the locals a chance and they'd have stripped your wreck within the hour." He saw Leslie's polite disbelief and used his pipe like an indignant pointer. "I'm being serious. Ask Thane. You'd need a cordon of cops standing shoulder to shoulder to be sure of protecting anything out there."

"He's right," admitted Thane wryly.

It wasn't much more than a week since a full-sized bull-dozer had somehow, still inexplicably, vanished from a Fortrose construction site in broad daylight. Later, when two Millside plainclothesmen had been sent out to collect a suspect, they'd returned empty-handed to their car to find all four wheels were missing. They reckoned it had been a bunch of twelve-year-olds they'd noticed hanging about.

"I'll accept your judgement," murmured Leslie in a very dry voice. "Perhaps the airport did seem safer—at the time."

Ilford gave a slight shrug but stayed silent and waited, his face giving nothing away.

"You mean something happened at the airport?" asked Thane, puzzled.

"Yes. But that's rushing things a little." Leslie's raw-boned face gave a slight smile which asked for patience and he gestured at the photographs again. "The Beagle isn't the newest of aircraft, but it's a sturdy, foolproof little machine with a good safety record. My job is to find out why this one crashed—try to find out, anyway."

"You take the wreck and put it together again, jigsaw style," nodded Thane. "I know."

"The same for any aircraft accident—we're technical scavengers, wanting to know why." Leslie nursed his hands together and cracked his knuckles with a mild embarrassment. "That way, maybe we can stop the same thing happening to some other poor basket, Thane. Except this time might be different. It looks like the pilot had been drinking."

"But he died a couple of hours ago without regaining consciousness," said Buddha Ilford curtly.

"And there are additional complications," added Leslie.

Thane gave a wary glance in Ilford's direction and the C.I.D. chief gave a fractional nod.

"The reason you're here," agreed Ilford. "The wreck was stowed in a hangar at the airport at 4 A.M., then Captain Leslie's team left to catch some sleep." He shrugged. "At 6 A.M., a wandering airport security man reached the hangar on his normal rounds. It was still dark, he thought he heard something happening inside, and the damned fool went in to take a look on his own."

"The next thing he really knows for sure is he was lying on the hangar floor with blood on his head and the vague notion he could hear a car driving off," said Leslie in a flat voice. "He'd been knocked out, probably for a few minutes."

"Somebody got in by forcing a rear window in the hangar," said Ilford. He stopped, fought his way through a short coughing bout, swore at himself, then added, "Nobody else saw anything, knows anything—at that hour, the whole airport was about as empty as a concrete desert."

Most airports were that way in the pre-dawn hours, before the first big passenger jets of the new day began warming up. Thane stayed silent a moment, his eyes straying to the ceiling. It was constructed of large white acoustic tiles and one of them had already sprung loose along two edges. Any new building had problems, but he reckoned that particular tile, if it fell, had a good chance of braining Ilford in the process. With a little luck, anyway.

"Anything missing?" he asked.

"I wish I knew," admitted Leslie. "But it looks as if someone searched through the Beagle's cockpit area. If there was something aboard he wanted, he must have got it, because I took a damned good look myself before I came over here."

"Nothing to do with the aircraft itself?"

"Petty pilfering?" The department man shook his head. "No, I don't think so." He took a glance at his wristwatch, carefully closed his briefcase, then got to his feet. "I've got to get back there now, Chief Inspector. But for what it's worth, I'll give you any help I can—though right now that isn't much."

He gave them a nod, said his good-byes, and left. Once the door had closed, Buddha Ilford sat silent for a long minute, contemplating his paunchy navel in the scowling style which had earned him his nickname for more than a decade.

Thane stayed quiet too, waiting. The spring sunlight was streaming in through the window behind the C.I.D. chief, somehow picking out the tired lines around his eyes and at the corners of his mouth. Suddenly it came to Thane that Buddha Ilford's hair was thinning fast and that his face had aged. It couldn't be the flu bug, it was more like the effects of strain. But then, the Strathclyde syndrome was no respecter of rank.

Buddha Ilford's face tightened at the same moment, almost as if he'd read Thane's mind. When he spoke, the usual whipcrack had returned behind the croak in his voice.

"I'm due at a meeting, Colin. But before you leave, get one thing straight in your mind."

"Sir?" Thane knew that when Ilford slipped into first name terms it mattered.

"The way this aircraft crashed in your division is incidental—I've other reasons for making it your case." Ilford laid one thick-fingered paw flat on his desk and gave a half-smile. "We may have got hold of something that matters, or it may not amount to a row of beans. Understand?"

Thane didn't, but nodded.

"Between the aircraft's movements and the rest, the thing sprawls all over the damned Strathclyde region. You'll be barging across a lot of the old county boundaries, including one or two places where the local cops are still manning the barricades."

"And if I meet a barricade, what do I do?" asked Thane. "Kick it down?"

He understood a lot more now. There were odd guerilla pockets of police resistance up and down the region, local men still being Awkward Annies and loathing the rapid changes around them. But the idea of being sent out to preach the gospel of Strathclyde alarmed him.

"Make it a Strathclyde case—show them the system works. Or at least make it look that way. I'm relying on your usual thick-skinned lack of diplomacy—and that's all I'm saying." Ilford picked up a thin manila folder and shoved it across the desk. "All we've got on the crash is in there. I want it wrapped up quickly, smoothly, neatly."

Thane took the folder and rose. He glanced up at the acoustic tile above Ilford's head, wishing it would fall there and then.

"I know, but it won't," said Ilford. He tried to grin and coughed instead. "This damned virus is more likely to finish me. Colin, something else before you go."

"Sir?"

"Advice, off the record." Ilford's broad face suddenly lost all expression. "Despite what I said, make sure you keep your nose spotlessly clean on this." Deliberately, he flicked over a few pages of his diary. "You know, I've got a damned Promotions Board meeting due at the end of the month. Life's full of little surprises, isn't it?"

Thane met his gaze for a moment and kept his own face equally expressionless.

"Keep in touch," said Ilford.

Then he gave a slight nod, ending the interview, and reached for his intercom telephone.

The file on the Beagle crash said that the pilot had been thirty-two-year-old Manuel Francis, an experienced private pilot who held I.M.C. and night ratings. Francis, a bachelor, was a travel agency manager in the city and had lived in a couple of rooms above his office. His passenger, Anna Harris, aged twenty-eight, divorced, had been employed by the same firm, Eurobreak Vacations, as a secretary and courier. By an odd quirk, her home had been on the edge of Millside Division.

The Beagle had been hired at Glasgow Airport on the Sunday morning. From there, Francis and his passenger had flown north to Glenfinn, a grass airstrip in the North Argyll hills where a local flying club operated.

Glenfinn was about forty minutes away by air. The Beagle had landed there at noon and had stayed parked there all afternoon and evening. It wasn't till after 1 A.M. that two of the flying club members had seen Francis and the girl leave again.

It had looked a routine take-off. Later, approaching Glasgow, Francis had confirmed with normal radio procedures and had acknowledged instructions as he was fed into the normal airport approach pattern, being brought round over the edge of the city to line up for a final visual landing on runway two-four.

Then, suddenly, there had been silence. And the Beagle's blip had disappeared from the radar screens.

There were other documents in the file. Closing it and laying it aside, Colin Thane knew plenty of people had already been busy.

He eased into a more comfortable position on the tall laboratory stool and tried to be patient. After he had left Ilford, he had made one telephone call to Millside Division which should have started some fresh wheels moving, then had come straight to the Headquarters forensic laboratory.

The reason had been yet another of the notings in the file. A blood sample had been taken from Manuel Francis at the same time as he'd been connected to a hospital plasma drip.

Now the blood sample was number twelve in a carousel of thirty numbered bottles clicking and purring their way round the laboratory's F.40 magic roundabout. Two other carousels, similarly loaded, were waiting their turn.

Each sample bottle was partly filled with prepared blood. Each sample—except for number twelve—represented a driver who had been breathalysed by police road patrols over the weekend. But as far as the F.40—the F.40 Multifract Gas Chromatograph, to give its full name—was concerned they were simply there to be analysed for blood alcohol content, the only job it was programmed to do.

The door behind Thane swung open. The man who came in wore a white laboratory coat, sported a dazzling red and yellow bow tie, and had a small, dark beard.

"Coffee," he said, setting down two mugs. "Our own brew." Casually, he glanced over at the F.40. "You're getting near the head of the queue."

Thane sipped from one of the mugs and nodded. Matthew Amos was the new forensic laboratory's assistant director and a civilian. Most of the new laboratory team were civilians, but in Amos's case the correct description was an aggressive civilian.

On the day he arrived, Matthew Amos had pinned a magazine picture of Che Guevara on his office wall, then had gone around declaring he wanted to inspect everyone's union card. Even Special Branch still weren't sure whether it had been done purely to annoy.

But Matt Amos knew his job and once in that white coat he was as impartial as a steel rule.

Or as the F.40. Another sample bottle, number eleven, clicked into its maw. The whole process was automatic, the F.40 linked to a small computer which translated the chromatograph readings and a teletype which had just finished spitting out the previous sample's result.

"This one was stoned out of his mind," said Amos, checking the print-out. "Look at it—320 milligrams alcohol per hundred millilitres blood. But what's the bet he'll claim he only had a couple of beers with the boys?"

"We had a character who blamed his new toothpaste," said Thane absently. "Matt, how about pilots who drink?"

"I avoid them," said Amos. "I get worried enough with the sober ones." Then the humour switched out of his voice. "Most commercial airlines put a complete ban on booze for twelve hours before a pilot takes a flight—and the quickest way known for a pilot to lose his licence is liquor, thank God."

"Stay dry if you want to fly?" asked Thane.

"Uh-huh. But ask a lawyer if you want chapter and verse," said Amos, taking a gulp of coffee. "Remember, I'm simply the mechanic around here."

"I never forget it," said Thane.

The bearded "mechanic" in front of him had come from

a top university research team, direct. Not for extra money —in the police, that would have been almost a laugh in itself—but because he had found the cloistered life boring.

The F.40 clicked again. Sample bottle number twelve, the blood from the late Manuel Francis, came into position. A small piston raised the bottle up, a fine steel hypodermic needle stabbed down through the bottle's seal, and an exact quantity of the head-space vapour was drawn off without the blood being touched.

Like every other bottle, number twelve had been preheated to a constant temperature before it reached the needle. The whole system was automatically cleansed before the next bottle could come round—and from the moment a loaded carousel was placed in position no human agency was involved. Using pre-set programmes, the F.40 could work away long after the last of the forensic laboratory staff had gone home.

That happened often enough. An average of nine thousand Road Traffic Act blood alcohol samples were fed to it each year, meaning nine thousand drivers from the city and around whose licences and sometimes liberty depended on those print-out readings.

"Here we go," said Amos, as the teletype burst into another brief chatter. He leaned forward, interested, then glanced at Thane. "Like a guess?"

"I'll pick positive," said Thane.

"You've just won today's star prize," agreed Amos, tearing the print-out sheet from the teletype. "We'll report 140 milligrams per 100 millilitres. You know how it goes—if he'd been driving a car, 80 milligrams is the permitted maximum."

"Would it have shown?"

"He wasn't drunk, but I'd have taken a parachute. His co-ordination would be frayed at the edges—well frayed."

The door swung open again and another white coat entered the room. The girl was small and pretty and Chinese. She was also a sub-inspector in the Hong Kong police force who had just taken a master of science degree at Glasgow University and was now on six-month attachment before going home.

"Matt," she said apologetically, looking worried, "can you spare a moment? I've blown a fuse or something."

"Again?" Amos grinned. "Colin, believe me, Eastern Promise has nothing on this one. Hand her a screwdriver and it becomes a deadly weapon." He winked at the girl. "Still, old Chinese proverb. I fix now, I collect later."

"Another old Chinese proverb," she retorted. "Get knotted."

"Good-bye, Colin," said Amos. "I'll send on the official report. He started for the door, then paused. "You should have got me a sample from his passenger. That way, we'd have known if they'd both had a happy time."

The late Manuel Francis had managed the Eurobreak Vacations office in Fidus Street, which was in an old, ugly part of Northern Division territory. But it was a good location. Fidus Street might sag on the property market, but there were two large factories just around the corner, each with a considerable labour force, and factory hands arranged holidays like everyone else.

The Eurobreak office, one of a row of shops with rooms above, presented a bright, prosperous front to the world around. The windows were filled with poster displays offering bargain flights to Switzerland and the Mediterranean, backed by the usual photographs of bikini-clad girls with sun-tanned navels.

Thane arrived in Fidus Street aboard the Millside duty car at 11 A.M. His head ached and his throat was raw and all the way over the car radio had been making hysterical noises about an armed hold-up over on the south side of Glasgow. But he felt slightly happier when he saw another police car parked near the Eurobreak offices.

He got out, told the duty-car driver not to wait, and once the car had gone he went straight into a chemist's shop two doors along. He bought a tube of aspirin, swallowed a couple at the counter, then walked along to the Eurobreak office. A uniformed constable was yawning behind the wheel of the parked police car and Thane gave him a nod. Constable Erickson, a big, blond Viking of a man, grinned back. He had a book on his lap, as usual—Erickson's off-duty time was divided equally between girls and law classes, and when he actually slept was a Millside mystery.

Pushing open the travel agency door, Thane went in. The only customer in sight was a woman carrying a small dog. She was collecting brochures from a display and talking earnestly to the dog before each choice. On the other side of the counter, a pretty, red-haired girl in her early twenties switched on a smile as Thane got there. But her eyes were red, as if she'd been crying earlier, and the smile switched off as Thane silently showed her his warrant card.

"Through here," she said, lifting a counter flap.

Thane followed her to a frosted glass door marked MAN-AGER. She opened it, waved him in, then closed the door behind him again as he entered.

There were already three men in the room, two seated and one standing. The man standing was young and thin and smartly dressed, while an older man, prematurely white-haired and in a dark business suit, frowned up at Thane from the nearest chair. But Thane's glance went first to the scrawny, untidy figure who grinned at him from the opposite side of the room.

"How's the flu bug?" asked Detective Inspector Phil Moss. "I thought they'd bring you in an ambulance."

"I'm being heroic about it," Thane told him with hoarse sarcasm. "Wait till it's your turn."

Phil Moss, second-in-command at Millside C.I.D., stayed amused. He was a small, grey, rake-thin man somewhere in his middle fifties. As usual, he looked as though he had slept in his clothes and if he'd shaved at all the razor blade had jumped a few times. Brand-new beat cops had been known to try to move him on as a vagrant, then been left with his acid invective burned deep into their souls. He also had a stomach ulcer famed throughout every police division in the city and which he guarded against anything resembling a doctor.

"I'd better handle the introductions," said Moss. At the same time he gave a fractional headshake, meaning Thane had missed nothing that particularly mattered. "I already explained you were on your way over."

The white-haired man was John Peebles, Eurobreak's managing director. He had a flabby handshake, he didn't bother to get out of his chair, and his hard, dark eyes went with a gold filling in a front tooth and a heavy platinum identity bracelet on his left wrist.

The second man, Peter Ellison, also shook hands. He was an account executive with the agency, looked about thirty, wore a corduroy suit in dark brown with a matching tie and shirt, and had a beak-nosed face that would have been handsome except for a deep pitting left by acne.

"We came straight over from our main office this morning when we heard," explained Peebles in a slow-paced, rich voice which held a vibration of regret. "One of the staff here called me—and it's a tragedy of course. Two employees dead, both people we liked."

"Were you surprised they had been together?" asked Thane innocently.

Peebles shrugged, his well-tailored suit rippling smoothly. Then he glanced at Ellison.

"Manny Francis collected girls like they were trading stamps," said Ellison. "Having a bird like Anna Harris on the doorstep must have been like a job satisfaction bonus to him—she had looks."

"Not after the crash," said Thane quietly.

"So I understand." John Peebles looked embarrassed and glared at Ellison. "Ah—what caused the crash, Chief Inspector?"

Thane shook his head. "That's someone else's worry."

"Inspector Moss suggested Manny had been on the booze," said Ellison, still unperturbed. "What about it?"

"It looks that way," said Thane. "Would you say he was a heavy drinker?"

"If he had been, he wouldn't have stayed working for me," said John Peebles. "Everybody cuts loose now and again—that's different."

"And he did?" asked Thane.

Peebles frowned. "Not when he was due to fly, and I've been up with him myself. Of course, having the girl along with him—"

"That's when the rules might go to hell," said Moss, who had been staying silent.

"It happens." Peebles ran a hand over his thick white hair and grimaced a little. "Well, we'll never know, I suppose. For now, I'm leaving Ellison in temporary charge here—though I can't really spare him from head office. Things may look quiet outside, but this branch is busy all year round."

"So you'll miss Francis," said Thane.

"That's an understatement." Peebles rose and collected his coat from a peg. "Contact me any time if you need help, Thane." He paused while he shrugged his way into the coat then asked softly, "Tell me one thing. Is there something special about this plane crash?"

"Meaning?" Thane raised an eyebrow and looked puzzled.

"Legwork like this—and a Chief Inspector turns out. I'm wondering why." The white-haired man waited, the platinum identity bracelet jingling on his wrist as he brought out his car keys.

"We could be interested in Manuel Francis," said Thane carefully. "If anything firms, we'll let you know."

"You'd better," said Peebles. He signalled Ellison, and the younger man followed him out of the room. The door closed firmly behind them and as it did, Phil Moss released a rumbling belch.

"God," he said. "That's better."

Thane grinned. Moss's ulcer behaved like a barometer, particularly when its owner forgot about things like eating regularly. But it also gave a guide to how Moss's nervous tension stood.

"Friend Peebles got you worried?" he asked. "Or is it his little friend?"

"Them?" Moss snorted. "They may be hard men in the package-trip world, but I'm not going anywhere."

"Then?"

"I took a look through Francis's apartment up above. The morning mail was lying behind the door." He reached into his pocket, dragged out an envelope, and handed it over. "That was among it."

Thane opened the envelope. Inside was a folded account on a florist's billhead. He glanced at the details then, puzzled, turned to Moss again.

"Why did he buy a funeral wreath?"

"The usual reason," said Moss. "Someone died. According to the little redhead outside, Francis was at a funeral three days ago."

"All right, let's have it," said Thane. "Who had the star role?"

"A friend of his, another weekend pilot." Moss eyed him deadpan. "Would you believe this one fell out of a window?"

"The way I feel, I'd believe anything." Thane brought out his cigarettes, took one, tossed another across to Moss, and they shared a light from a chrome table lighter on the desk. "Better check it out, Phil."

"I will." Moss let his cigarette dangle from his mouth, the first flakes of ash dusting his jacket lapels. "The girl says his name was Ben Cassill, an office supplies agent—"

"Who just fell from a window." Thane sighed. The cigarette tasted like a gorilla's bedsock, which was probably the flu bug's fault. The old, hoary couplet "did he fall or was he pushed" drifted wearily through his mind. "Happy Monday, Phil."

"Eh?" Moss blinked.

"Forget it," said Thane. "Show me where Francis lived."

This time, he told himself gloomily, Assistant Chief Constable William "Buddha" Ilford had really dropped him in it. Even without the threatened Promotions Board.

CHAPTER TWO

The living quarters above the Eurobreak Vacations branch office were reached by a back stairway and amounted to a large lounge, a bedroom, a well-equipped kitchen and a tiny bathroom. As they entered, Moss switched on the concealed strip lighting then Thane took a first look around. The bed was unmade and there were used breakfast dishes lying in the kitchen sink, where Manuel Francis must have left them the previous day. Otherwise the apartment was tidy and the furnishings were expensive. The tourist agency manager had enjoyed his creature comforts.

"He had a woman come to clean three mornings a week," said Moss, standing in the middle of the lounge. "Otherwise he was on his own—no problems."

Thane grinned. Phil Moss lived in a South Side boardinghouse where his landlady, a widow, kept the rent low and her hopes high. She also fought a continuing, despairing battle to prevent her star boarder going out looking as if he'd fallen off a dust-cart.

"Find anything that matters?" he asked.

"No surprises. But I didn't know what I was trying to find—and I still don't."

"That makes two of us," said Thane. One of the concealed lighting tubes had a fault and the hum coming from it was boring into his skull. He went through to the kitchen, took a glass from a cupboard, filled it with water and drank deeply. "How about personal stuff?"

"A wardrobe full of clothes, a bankbook with a couple of thousand pounds in credit, a passport with more visa stamps than I've had hot dinners—" Moss grimaced. "He was doing all right."

"Till his luck ran out." Thane set down the glass.

"Like you say." Moss belched in a lower key and fumbled in his top pocket. Out came a grubby handkerchief and from the middle of it he produced a large, equally grubby bismuth tablet which he put in his mouth and began sucking. Watching the performance, Thane decided that between them they would have made any medical practitioner's day.

They went back into the lounge. An expensive stereo outfit dominated most of one wall and beside it a framed photograph stood on top of a teak storage cabinet. It showed a smiling, dark-haired man in sports clothes standing beside an open car.

"Francis?" asked Thane.

Moss nodded and took a closer look. Manuel Francis had been slim, medium height, and reasonably good-looking. His smile held the easy confidence of a man who hadn't a particular care in the world.

"How much liquor did he keep around, Phil?"

"Two or three bottles in a cupboard," said Moss, flopping down in an armchair. "That's all—if he was a real drinking man, he hid the empties."

Thane crossed to a small mahogany sideboard, where a stylised model of a light aircraft made in clear glass lay glinting on the dark wood. It was an attractive ornament and he pursed his lips appreciatively when he lifted it and saw the small label on the base. It read Eaglefarm Crafts. He remembered being window shopping with Mary once when she'd seen a glass fox ornament which she had liked. They'd priced it—the fox had been made by Eaglefarm and the cost had been beyond their budget.

"Exactly what are we looking for anyway?" persisted Moss from the depths of the armchair.

"Ideas. We need them." Thane laid the glass aircraft back in place.

"All because an amateur pilot drinks too much and crashes? Look, the business about the security man being thumped on the head could be coincidence. Some airport prowler out for kicks and—"

He stopped there. Thane had opened the top drawer of the chest and was standing looking down at it in a way that didn't need a crystal ball to interpret. Rising, Moss went over to join him.

"What's up?" he asked.

Silently, Thane pointed to the small brass lock in the middle of the drawer and the wood around it. Both were badly scratched and the tongue of the lock rattled loosely when he touched it with a finger.

"Hell," said Moss softly. He took a closer look. "Well, I missed that. Sorry."

"That kind of lock could be forced with a penknife. Anytime—now or years ago." Thane opened the drawer wider. It contained a collection of old cheque stubs, filed bills, and other bits and pieces of paper—the kind of collection most people had somewhere. Shrugging, he closed the drawer again. "How did you get in here when you arrived?"

"There was a spare key on a hook downstairs, beside the

other office keys." Looking chastened, Moss reached into a pocket and produced it, along with the remains of a half-eaten bar of chocolate. "Do we go back down and—?"

"No." Thane shook his head slowly. "We'll say nothing. Not till we've better reason." He gave Moss a lopsided grin. "Forget it, Phil. If someone did come up here, it helps—you aren't the only one who needs encouragement."

There was nothing else in the apartment that showed any sign of having been tampered with—they made sure of that in the next few minutes.

Then, closing and locking the apartment door behind them, they went back down to the travel agency. Peter Ellison was in the manager's office, sitting at Manuel Francis's desk with a stack of account files in front of him and a pocket calculator at his fingertips.

"Finished?" asked Ellison, his pock-marked face creasing in a hopefully polite greeting.

"For now." Thane considered a travel poster on the wall, a four-colour hard sell for the Italian Riviera. "How are things in the travel trade?"

"Like John Peebles said, we're busy. He's the boss—he should know." Ellison sat back, shoving his hands deep into the pockets of his brown corduroy jacket. "All our branch figures are up on last year. Including here—business is good."

"But you're making sure." Thane glanced deliberately at the folders. "Whose idea was it?"

"I do what I'm told, don't you?"

"How well did you know Manny Francis?"

Ellison shrugged. "He ran the branch, I came over from head office now and again—and we had a drink together a couple of times." His eyes narrowed slightly. "But before you ask, we didn't go out and get stoned together. That's not my style."

"How long had he been with Eurobreak?" asked Moss, leaning against the edge of the desk.

"Since the start, longer than I've been." He saw they wanted more and sighed. "John Peebles founded the firm from scratch three years back, and Manny was one of the original hands. That was in the small-time days—now we've got head office and half a dozen branches." Ellison paused and thumbed over his shoulder at the poster. "There's the secret, our speciality. Low-budget holidays for the toiling masses. There are a hell of a lot of them around."

"I've noticed," said Thane. "How does it pay?"

"Well enough. We handle the complete package. Travel, hotels, excursions, discount souvenirs—even sell them the foreign currency they're going to need. I'll bet Manny Francis was drawing more than you make, Chief Inspector, and as a branch manager he got commission on top of salary."

"Did Francis ever talk about relatives or friends?" asked Moss.

Ellison shook his head.

"What about a man called Cassill, another spare-time pilot—ever hear of him?"

"No, sorry."

"Then girls," suggested Thane patiently. "We found the makings of a pin-up gallery upstairs."

"Trophies, I'd imagine." Ellison dismissed them. "Manny played the field, made sure he never got in too deep."

"With Anna Harris the last of the line?" Thane felt his throat drying up again but kept on. "How long had she been working here?"

"Since last summer—at least, that's when she came on the payroll," answered Ellison. "She started as a travel courier on our Spanish package tours and spoke the lan-

guage like a native. We usually pay off our couriers at the
end of season, but John Peebles gave her a home-based job
for the winter. He reckoned she was too good to lose."

Thane raised an eyebrow. "Was that the only reason?"

"I'd say yes." Ellison opened a desk drawer and began
rummaging in it. "He's the kind who gets his kicks from
making money. Women don't particularly turn him on,
and I don't mean he's bent. Anyway, Anna Harris was
worth it. We've used her in our new season's brochure."

He produced a colour printed folder from the drawer,
spread it out on the desk, and pointed to a photograph on
the front cover.

"That's her."

The photograph showed a blond girl with wide-eyed
good looks and a slim, near-perfect figure. She was in a
smartly cut courier uniform and waved a greeting from the
top step into a jumbo jet. Thane's lips tightened as he
thought of what he'd seen in the crash photographs.

"Will you keep her on the cover?" asked Moss.

"That's a problem." Ellison frowned. "Reprinting would
cost money—anyway, it's a good picture and John Public
has a short memory. But it won't be my decision." He considered the photograph again, almost sadly. "I'm married—
that ruled me out. But she was the kind of girl you don't
forget."

Thane nodded, believing him.

"Keep it." Ellison gave him the folder. "We did a print
run of thirty thousand. Anything else?"

"No," Thane tucked the folder into an inside pocket.
"But we'll be back, and his apartment will have to stay
locked."

"If you say so." Ellison showed no particular interest.

Rising, he went to the door which led to the front office. "But we close at six and the only way to Manny's place is through the office. He had his own keys."

Phil Moss glanced at Thane and gave a fractional nod. Everything from the dead man's pockets was now in a plastic bag at the city mortuary, waiting collection.

"Another thing," said Ellison as he opened the door and they went out, "if we've a holiday package that interests either of you, let me know. Eurobreak would be happy to arrange a special concession rate." He eyed them blandly. "Of course, we like a good public image—you'll understand that."

"I'd be surprised if you didn't," said Thane.

Ellison smiled and nodded then he closed the door on them. Left glaring at the door, Moss gave a growl.

"This week's special offer," he said.

"I know. Keep Eurobreak's image clean and we'll give you the five-star-hotel treatment. Relax, Phil. If he tries it again I'll boot him up the tail."

"Take the offer first, then boot him," suggested Moss. He glanced along the front office towards the public counter. "There's the girl who told me about Francis and that wreath."

It was the young redhead who had spoken to Thane when he arrived. They passed a clerk selling a cruise to an elderly dowager, reached the redhead, and she abandoned another customer, opening the counter flap to let them out.

"What's your name?" asked Thane pleasantly.

"Jenny Baird." She was in her early twenties and looked as though she wished they'd keep on going.

"Mind if I talk to you about Anna Harris?" asked Thane. "How well did you know her?"

"We got on." She flushed to the roots of her red hair. "I wouldn't say she was a close friend."

"Did you know she was planning to go flying with Francis?"

The girl nodded. "She told me on Friday. They'd been out together a few times."

"Flying?" asked Moss.

"Sometimes." She glanced along at her customer, who was waiting patiently. "I think they usually went up to Glenfinn."

"Any reason for that?"

"I don't think so." She frowned. "I think Mr. Francis just liked going there."

"And now they're dead." Thane made a sympathetic noise. "How strong did you think things were between them?"

"You mean was it special?" She flushed a deeper red. "Manny—Mr. Francis wasn't built that way. Anyway, Anna always said one divorce behind her was enough. She'd nothing against men, but she wasn't going to tie herself down again, ever."

Thane smiled, with a feeling Jenny Baird had also been through the Manny Francis process at some time.

"Did his friend Ben Cassill ever come here?"

"Now and again." The customer along the counter was making impatient noises and she fidgeted. "Sometimes we ordered a few office supplies from him, but I think he really just looked in to see Mr. Francis."

"I just wondered." Thane paused, then made it sound like an afterthought. "Incidentally, who opened up the office this morning?"

"I did." She looked puzzled. "I've got a set of main-door

keys—sometimes Mr. Francis wakened late. It was a private arrangement."

"The kind head office didn't know about?" He nodded his understanding. "Everything was normal when you came in?"

"Yes." The girl's puzzlement grew. "Why?"

"We get paid for asking idiot questions," said Moss cheerfully. "There's a report form for everything these days."

They let her go back to her customer and went out of the travel agency. The light wind was blowing rubbish along the grey street and a cloud had covered the sun. Thane caught himself shivering as they walked along to the Millside Division car.

"What's next?" asked Moss.

"Anna Harris's place." Thane shivered again, conscious that his mind felt like a wad of wet cotton, then saw Moss's face. "What the hell are you grinning at?"

"I'm not." Moss's acid grin widened. "But you look rough. How would you like my cool hand on your fevered brow?"

"You'd have to wash it first," said Thane.

The insult didn't even dent Phil Moss's amusement.

It was a ten-minute drive across the city to their next stop, and that took them back inside the front of Millside Division territory. Anna Harris had lived in a one-time Victorian mansion in Balfour Street which time and necessity had seen converted into a block of service flats. Most of the other big houses around had gone the same way, their faded frontages a sad reminder of a previous moneyed elegance which had moved on.

"Don't forget the boffin box, Erickson," said Thane as their big, blond driver brought the Jaguar to a halt at the kerb. "God might think we've got lost."

Erickson grinned, leaned over, and tapped two buttons on the shiny new Cyfax box screwed in position under the instrument panel. Every Strathclyde mobile working in the city had a Cyfax box now—it linked by radio with the big Ferranti Military systems computer at Headquarters, automatically updating a car's position on the Command Control visual display screens. It made for rapid switching of mobile units to incident locations, but it still left a feeling that Big Brother was watching.

"You know what should happen?" asked Moss querulously from the rear seat. "We should get every mobile to punch the same buttons at the same moment. What would that do, eh?"

"Signal overload," said Erickson. "It could be interesting. I think—"

Moss cut him short with a despairing growl. They left Erickson considering the possibility, got out of the car, and walked up a narrow path through an overgrown tangle of garden to the front door of the one-time mansion. An elderly caretaker, a small, garrulous man with a grey moustache and blue overalls, answered the doorbell and let them in.

"Expected the cops would be along. They gave her name on the radio news this mornin'—so what kept you till now?"

"Didn't you want time to get over your grief?" asked Thane frostily. He didn't bother to wait for an answer. "Got a key to her place?"

The man nodded, beckoned, and toiled ahead of them up three flights of cheaply carpeted stairway. Stopping at the top landing, he brought out a master key and opened the door to Anna Harris's apartment.

"Good enough tenant," he said, leaning against the doorway. "I'll stay here, right? I'm responsible if anythin' goes missing."

They brushed past him and began looking through the apartment. It was smaller than Manny Francis's place and totally feminine from the laundered underwear draped to dry on the bathroom radiator to the litter of make-up on the bedroom dressing table. Nothing seemed disturbed and it was the same in the living room, which had a tiny kitchen leading off it.

"See those?" The caretaker joined them and pointed at two Spanish bullfight posters pinned to the wall above a television set. "I was on holiday in Spain mysel' once—saw a bullfight too. The matador bloke got a horn up his rear an' the local punters loved it." He produced a crumpled cigarette from his top pocket, cupped his hands round a match, then leered at them through the first puff of smoke. "She tol' me she'd worked in Spain for a spell."

Thane ignored him. A miniature stag's head modelled in glass was staring at them from a display shelf near the window. When he picked it up and turned it over, another Eaglefarm Crafts label was on the underside. He put the stag's head down again and turned to face the caretaker.

"When did you see her last?"

The old man chewed one end of his moustache. "Saturday afternoon—I had t' come up and fix a new washer on a tap for her." He winked at them. "Wanderin' around in a dressin' gown she was, with damn all under it that I could see."

"Just as well you're past the age of caring," said Moss. "You said she was a good tenant?"

"Paid her rent, didn't make trouble—not like some in this place. If I ever did her a favour, then she slipped me somethin' for beer money. God knows what the next one in here will be like. There's some real rubbish wanderin' around Glasgow these days."

"How about men friends?" asked Moss, flicking through the message pad which lay beside a cream telephone.

"She brought one back now an' again—nobody regular." The old man watched them with a sudden caution. "None of my business, was it? I mean, there are half a dozen unattached females in this block. If they want to have a bit o' bed-rumple now an' again, that's natural, isn't it?"

"And more beer money if you forget it," said Moss. "Any special friends among the other tenants?"

"Nope." The caretaker had a sudden thought. "Here, if you're stuck for someone to identify the body, I could do that. You get paid, right?"

"Wrong," said Thane, and thumbed towards the door. "Out. We're leaving and so are you. Nobody else gets in here unless they show a warrant card first, understand?"

On the way to the door he reached for the aspirin bottle in his pocket, palmed two more aspirin, and swallowed them. He waited on the landing with Moss till the caretaker had locked the door again.

"Don't I get anythin' for my trouble?" he complained.

Moss looked him up and down and belched, then followed Thane down the stairway towards the street.

As soon as they were back aboard the divisional car, Thane told Erickson to head for Millside police office. Then, as the car started and pulled away from the kerb he turned to Moss.

"I'll drop you off, Phil, then take the airport on my own."

"Suits me." Moss yawned, but his eyes weren't sleepy. "I'm due a lunch break. What do you want me to do?"

Thane told him, while the car purred on through the busy streets and the sun broke through the last edge of the grey clouds that had been overhead.

They needed a full run-down on the Eurobreak agency's background, with particular attention to John Peebles and Ellison. The same, even more so, applied to Manny Francis and Anna Harris, while the division that had handled the death of Francis's friend Ben Cassill could supply details from their own report sheets.

"Do we get the forensic squad to look around Manny Francis's place?" asked Moss. He brought out his half-eaten chocolate bar and nibbled at an edge. "Without a fuss, I mean."

"If they can do it that way," agreed Thane. He had to stop to clear his throat, which felt like sandpaper again. "I'd like a woman's view of the Harris girl's place too."

Moss grinned. The average cop couldn't tell Chanel from disinfectant. He added chasing the aircrash post-mortem reports to his mental list then raised an eyebrow at Thane's final item.

"Contact the local cops at Glenfinn. Say we'd appreciate them checking on what happened at their end before Francis took off for Glasgow last night." Like a punctuation mark, the Jaguar dropped a gear and accelerated for a moment to overtake a bulky truck and trailer. As the engine settled back to a purr again, he added, "Handle them gently, Phil. They're usually a prickly bunch in the Highlands."

"You're damned lucky if the average Highland cop admits he understands English," muttered Moss. "Right. Are you coming back in after the airport?"

Thane nodded. "Soon as I can. So if Buddha Ilford calls from Headquarters, stall him. Make the usual soothing noises."

"Yes sir, no sir," said Moss. He finished the chocolate bar, crumpled the wrapping, then saw Erickson glancing back at him through the rear mirror. He winked at the driver, deliberately stuffed the wrapping down the side of the seat, then settled back and closed his eyes.

By the time they dropped Moss at Millside Police Station it was noon. The divisional office wasn't a particularly impressive landmark. It was a grimy, stone-fronted slab of mock-Gothic architecture and brick extensions with a surround of waste ground. Most of the old slum tenement buildings which had once stood around it had been demolished and only the rats had objected. As the police car pulled away again, and passed other tenements farther down the street, which still clung to existence, the sight gave Thane an idea which meant a change of plan. He thought about it for a moment, then turned to Erickson as the car stopped at a set of traffic lights at the end of the street.

"Make it Fortrose first," he ordered. "I want to go back to the beginning."

Erickson didn't look pleased, thinking of his tyres. Streets in Fortrose were usually frosted with broken glass. But as the lights changed to green, he swung the steering wheel obediently.

It was another ten-minute ride, through streets which switched from shopping to industrial, back to shops and a thin suburban strip, then, finally, the high-rise, low-rent blocks which had been Glasgow's frantic answer to a housing crisis. In the process, it had also been the laying down of a new inheritance of social disaster. Fortrose was a monument to a well-meant failure, a lesson in the perils of dumping people into architect-designed filing cabinets and expecting the result to be an instant community.

A blue and white police Panda car cruised towards them near the first high-rise block. Erickson flashed his lights in a greeting and the solitary cop in the Panda flashed back as he passed and grinned.

A cop on a Fortrose beat hadn't much to grin about, thought Thane. They passed a huddle of shops, steel grilles permanently on the windows because that way the glass didn't get smashed. Further on, two teen-agers were making a leisurely business of kicking a third teen-ager they had down on the pavement. They saw the car and ran. Erickson slowed, but the teen-ager who had been on the ground got up, gave a two-fingered gesture at the car, and staggered off.

"Animals," said Erickson harshly.

"Maybe your future clients if you get that law degree," Thane reminded him. "They're still people. Don't forget it."

Erickson slowed again as the next block came up then stopped the Jaguar at the kerb with the engine ticking over. Thane looked out at the raw-edged scars on the wide grass verge, scars which marked where the crashed Beagle had come to rest. The high-rise block showed no sign of damage, the paint-sprayed slogan FORTIES RULE mocked him along the side of a nearby bus shelter.

"Sir." Erickson pointed towards the other side of the street. "We've an audience."

Thane nodded. Half a dozen local neds, most of them faces he'd seen often enough in the Millside Division charge room, were lounging in a group near a lamppost. Their unshaven faces were blank, they made no move, and he knew they'd stay that way till the car was gone. Neds—the city's term for small-time layabout criminals—had all the time in the world when it came to watching a visiting cop.

Unless they'd something to worry about, when they could disappear faster than a wisp of smoke.

"Happy Malloy, Billy Garrison, Doggy Spiers—" said Erickson, half to himself. "Who's the wee fellow in the tartan cap, sir?"

"Soldier Kelly," said Thane absently. The "Soldier" tag had stuck to Kelly ever since he'd spent two years on the run as an army deserter. "All right, let's end the entertainment."

They drove away. In a couple of minutes Fortrose had faded behind and Erickson swung the car into one of the feeder roads for the Clyde Tunnel. Once through the tunnel, south of the river, they were on the motorway route for Glasgow Airport.

Glasgow Airport was like anyone else's airport—a concrete and glass showbox structure which was the main terminal building then an untidy scatter of huts and hangars that fringed round most of the runways area. Erickson had to stop and ask directions a couple of times, but eventually they threaded through a network of service roads and stopped at one of the hangar buildings.

Thane stepped out of the car, into the sunlight, drew a deep breath, and ignored the burnt jet-fuel taste in the air. His throat wasn't so painful now and his head felt clearer. Either it was imagination, or the flu virus was in retreat.

"Tell Control we're off radio watch," he told Erickson, one hand still on the opened car door. "This could take time. Get yourself a sandwich if you want—but don't stray too far."

Erickson reached for the radio handset, humming under his breath. Leaving him, Thane made his way into the hangar, past a NO SMOKING sign. As soon as he was inside he heard the murmur of voices and saw a handful of men, most of them wearing overalls, working round the tangled wreckage that had been the four-seater Beagle Pup.

Thane went towards them, his footsteps loud on the bare concrete floor. As he passed the only other aircraft in the hangar, the old Dakota used for fire-squad training, two of the men left the wreckage of the Beagle and came to meet him while the others stopped work and stood waiting.

"Good timing," said Group Captain Leslie with a cheerful grin of welcome. The department accident inspector was in a white boiler suit which was smudged in places and he had a long, oily smear down one side of his raw-boned face. He sucked his teeth happily. "Yes, we're beginning to get somewhere with this one."

"They usually do," said his companion, a bulky, moon-faced police inspector with a uniform neat enough to have come straight from being cleaned and pressed. He eyed Thane with interest. "Headquarters told me you'd be along, Chief Inspector. I'm Dan Melrose, from the airport police sub-station."

Thane shook hands with the man, remembering the airport police were ex-county force and that plenty of them regarded themselves as stepchildren in the Strathclyde setup. But Melrose, who had close-clipped fair hair and light blue eyes, seemed friendly enough.

"Still trying to find your prowler?" Thane asked without

malice. "From what I heard, I wouldn't give much for your chances."

"That makes two of us," admitted Melrose.

"No outside witnesses?"

"None," said Melrose. "Like I told the assistant chief when he phoned—"

"Buddha Ilford?" asked Thane.

"Uh-huh. I told him an airport isn't like one of his Glasgow backstreets. He—hell, I still don't think he understands."

"That's possible," said Thane. He switched his attention back to Leslie. "Your pilot had been drinking, as you thought. His blood alcohol count was 140—we'd have had him if he'd been driving a car."

Leslie pursed his lips then led the way over to the wreckage. He stopped beside a crumpled section of wing, told the other men around to take a break, and waited till they had drifted away.

"How much do you know about aircraft, Thane?" he asked.

"Very little. It couldn't be much less," said Thane.

"Right." Leslie nodded at the wreckage. "This is a preliminary stage—the full treatment comes later. We've put the aircraft back together as near as we can, just to see what the pieces look like."

"Nothing missing?"

"Nothing that matters," said Leslie. "Like I told you, my job is to find out what happened then write a report. Among other things, it gets to other aircraft operators who can maybe learn from what went wrong. This time"—he sucked his teeth again—"everything shouts human error."

"Through drink?" asked Inspector Melrose.

"With blood-alcohol content and a resultant lowering in

pilot skills a major contributory factor," Leslie said in a mock-pompous fashion, then nodded. "Through a drink."

"How?" asked Thane.

"I'll show you," said Leslie.

He led Thane and the airport policeman on a brief guided tour of the spread-out wreckage, making noises about flap positions, altimeter settings, trim, engine status, and electrics.

"Now," said Leslie, "I'll come to what I think happened."

"Good," said Thane, exchanging a glance with Melrose. He was glad the airport policeman seemed equally baffled.

"The airport log shows Francis was being cleared for final approach. They advised him he was too low, and to gain another three hundred feet." Leslie shrugged. "We recovered the altimeter and the setting was three hundred feet out. His fault. He'd been given a revised altimeter setting when he entered controlled air space and contacted Glasgow by radio."

Thane frowned. "Then his instruments would read—"

"That he was three hundred feet higher than reality," said Leslie patiently. "Anyway, he began climbing. But air speed decreases in a climb unless you increase engine revolutions to match. If you don't"—he used a hand to illustrate—"you get to a point where the angle of attack is too great, where weight exceeds lift." His hand flopped down, the fingertips limp. "The nose drops. Your aircraft stalls, literally falls out of the sky."

"Because the engine stops?" Inspector Melrose's beefy red face showed his puzzlement.

"No. A car stalls when the engine stops," said Leslie with the air of a schoolteacher faced with a backward pupil. "An aircraft in a stall comes down with the engine still thrashing away." He shrugged, considering the crumpled, broken fuselage beside them. "The usual instrument warning light came on when his airspeed became critical—I found the switch still in the closed position. Once the stall warning comes on, either you act fast or the aircraft falls."

"But can't you counter a stall?" demanded Thane, the department man's words leaving him with a chill mental picture of two people tumbling out of the sky.

"Yes. It's basic training stuff." Leslie tapped a fragment of wing with one foot, gently. "Stick forward, nose down, power on—change your stall into a shallow dive, then pull out. But you've only seconds. Fumble, panic, and a wing drops, the aircraft starts to spin. You can still recover, and from the flap positions and instrument readings it looks like he tried. Except he was too late."

"Satan's eyeballs," said Inspector Melrose softly. "It's one hell of a way to die."

"Ask me about a flamer some time," said Leslie.

He glanced at Thane. "I'm near enough certain we can rule out anything except a pilot error accident. Though I'm not near the final report stage yet."

Thane nodded. "You know my basic interest. Did you check the cockpit area again?"

"I did better." Leslie gave a faint smile. "I brought in an airport Customs officer when I got back. He gave the whole plane a contraband-style search—and found nothing."

A telephone rang in a corner of the hangar. One of the group of men still waiting answered it, then shouted Leslie's name and beckoned.

"London, I expect," said Leslie unenthusiastically. "We all have bosses." He turned to go then paused another moment. "There's someone here who might interest you,

Thane. The ginger-haired youngster in the leather jacket—
he flew down from Glenfinn this morning."

Then he went off towards the telephone. His assistants
were drifting back again and Inspector Melrose had moved
away a few paces, standing with his hands in his pockets
and frowning at the wreckage. Thane looked around and
saw a tall, ginger-haired figure standing inconspicuously in
the shadows in a corner. He went over, while Leslie's technicians started work.

"I was told you'd flown down from Glenfinn," said
Thane.

"Right." The ginger-haired man gave him a friendly
nod. He was tall and freckle-faced and still in his early
twenties. "Gibby MacDonald's my name—police, aren't
you?"

"Does it show?" asked Thane.

"They said Chief Inspector." MacDonald gestured towards the technicians. He wore a yellow sweat shirt under
the leather jacket and was in faded blue denims. "I had to
bring a plane down from Glenfinn Flying Club for a main-
tenance check."

"Pre-arranged?"

MacDonald nodded and glanced towards the crumpled
Beagle. "I'm no sightseeing tourist. But I had to look in."

"You knew Francis?"

"We'd talked once or twice," said MacDonald carefully.
His freckled face was in need of a shave and he had a snub
nose and large ears which amounted to an oddly good-looking combination. "I'm an instructor at the Glenfinn Club.
That means I'm usually around at weekends."

Thane felt he'd been handed a mild bonus. "Did you
talk to him yesterday?"

"Yes. He said hello and not much more. He had the girl with him, they'd just parked the Beagle—and he didn't seem talkative. After the kind of landing he'd made, I'd have felt that way too."

"What was wrong with it?" asked Thane.

"He thumped the thing down like an old brick," said MacDonald. "Sort of thing you'd expect from a beginner—and he'd enough flying time to do better." He looked at the wreckage again, suddenly thoughtful. "Maybe—" he left it at that and shook his head.

"Did you see him after that?"

"No. I'd gone home before he took off again. A couple of the members did see him when he left." Again Mac-Donald seemed ready to say more but again he didn't.

"Something bothering you?" asked Thane quietly.

MacDonald sighed reluctantly. "Maybe if I'd been around I'd have tried to stop him taking off. The lads knew he'd been drinking, that he'd been in the bar at the local hotel, and it showed. He wasn't bad, but—"

"We know," said Thane. Leslie had finished his telephone call and was coming back towards them. "And there was an empty whisky flask in the cockpit."

"The stupid basket." MacDonald stared at him. "What made him do it?"

"It's a good question. Maybe someone at Glenfinn knows the answer." Thane made up his mind as he spoke. "I'll have to go there to find out."

"When?" MacDonald was immediately interested.

"Tomorrow sometime."

"Make it 8 A.M. and you can hitch a lift up with me. I'm stuck here till tomorrow—the crate I brought down needs more work done on it than I thought and the engineers say I can't have it back till morning."

Thane hesitated for more reasons than one. "How would I get back? I hadn't planned on staying."

"I'll fix that. Someone will fly you down again," Mac-Donald assured him. "No cost either way, so you'll save the ratepayers' money. Can you make it for eight?"

Thane gave in and nodded, deciding a friendly introduction might be useful in a Highland area like Glenfinn.

"I'll see you then," said MacDonald.

He ambled off, passing Leslie on the way. In another few seconds he had gone from the hangar.

"Was he any help?" Leslie asked Thane.

"Hard to tell yet, but I think so," said Thane. "What about your phone call?"

"Just London, like I thought." The department man grimaced. "A query about the last job I was on. Some armchair expert thought he'd caught us out." He dismissed the matter with a grunt then glanced at his wristwatch. "Time my people had a lunchbreak—union rules. I could use a sandwich myself. How about you?"

Thane nodded. The flu bug must still be on the retreat. He did feel slightly hungry, the shivering seemed to have stopped, and his head felt clearer.

"Right." Leslie raised his voice and shouted to the men working on the Beagle wreck. "Lunch break. Make it half an hour." As they stopped and began leaving the hangar in a group, Inspector Melrose came with them. Leslie beckoned him over. "Thane and I are going for a sandwich. How about you?"

Melrose hesitated, then shook his head.

"I've got to check at my office," he said. "I've a sergeant who'll be jumping up and down by now. But I'll walk over with you. Unless"—he frowned—"maybe I should get a man over to stand guard here."

"Stand guard on what?" asked Leslie dryly.

Melrose glanced at Thane, leaving it to him.

"Like he says," murmured Thane. "Why bother now?"

They were the last to leave the hangar. Outside, the Millside car stood empty in the bright sunlight and a British Airways shuttle jet, a Trident on the Glasgow-London run, was lifting from the main runway with a roar of thrust which put a halt to conversation. Behind it, a Spanish Aviaco charter flight and an Aer Lingus cargo plane were queuing for take-off.

There was a staff canteen block a few hundred yards away, hidden from sight behind an engineering shed. Melrose left them there, and Thane and Leslie went in. It was self-service, and they joined the small queue ahead of them.

"The food's good—and cheap enough," said Leslie almost apologetically, taking a tray and getting in line. "But if you wanted something better—"

"Your average police canteen doesn't specialise in haute cuisine," said Thane. He glanced at the menu on the wall. "In fact—"

It was as far as he got. The flat, low blast of an explosion cut him short, rattled every window in the canteen block, and stilled the conversation and clatter of dishes all around them.

"Hell," said Leslie, still clutching his tray. He stared, open-mouthed at Thane, then swallowed. "That sounded like it came from—"

Thane nodded. They dropped their trays and dashed out of the canteen block, conscious of others scrambling up from the tables to do the same. A moment later they rounded the corner of the engineering shed.

Thick smoke was billowing from the roof of the Beagle's hangar. As they ran on, a first tongue of yellow flame joined the smoke and somewhere behind them a fire siren had begun sounding.

Someone else was running, shouting as he went. It was Erickson, but the Millside driver was gesturing to them and heading away from the hangar. Cursing, Thane veered to join him as he realised why.

About two hundred yards ahead of Erickson another figure was sprinting hard. Thane put all he had into trying to close the gap, but first the pursued figure then Erickson disappeared round the corner of an office block.

Thane rounded the same corner an instant later and saw Erickson had stopped just ahead. Then he heard the driver's warning bellow at the same time as a small green Ford car started moving and came straight for them, engine howling through the gears.

Erickson had his baton out. He hurled it hard at the Ford's windscreen then dived clear. Thane had a glimpse of part of the windscreen shattering and of a stocking-masked figure hunched behind the wheel, then it was his turn to leap for his life as the car roared past.

It went into a screaming tyre-skid at the corner, then roared away.

While Erickson picked himself up from the ground Thane ran back to the end of the block. He was in time to see the green car speeding down a service road, then swinging out onto the main highway.

"I'll get back and use the radio," said Erickson as he limped over to join Thane. "I got the number—"

"So?" Thane shrugged at the uselessness of it. "We'll find the car abandoned two minutes away from here and it'll be on the stolen list." He glared at Erickson, whose uniform was smeared with dirt from taking his dive. "Where the hell were you anyway?"

"Watching the planes." Erickson flushed. "I thought—"

"We all thought. Where did he come from—the hangar?"

Erickson nodded. "Just before that bang. I saw him and started running, sir."

"Next time try harder," snarled Thane. Then he shook his head. "All right, call it square. I said the place didn't need a guard."

"You—uh—went off somewhere too," Erickson reminded him.

"That's right," said Thane coldly. "Don't just stand there, man. Go and play with your damned radio."

Fifteen minutes later the last of the airport fire tenders drew away from the smoke-blackened hangar, their task completed. Inside, Colin Thane splashed gloomily through the carpet of foam and water which covered the hangar floor and glanced at Captain Leslie as they stopped beside the charred, skeletal remains of the crashed Beagle Pup.

"Kerosene," said the department man in a professionally detached voice that was his way of keeping the lid on hysteria. "You know they found the can?"

Thane nodded. Inspector Melrose and his airport squad had it. By now it was probably on its way to the forensic laboratory at Headquarters.

He looked again at what was left of the Beagle. It had been gutted from nose to tail and the stench of its burning still laced the smoky air. If there had been anything hidden aboard the Beagle it must be lost for ever now.

"Well, he came back after all," said Leslie in the same flat voice. "Persistent. I'll give him that."

"He came back," agreed Thane.

The green Ford had been found abandoned half a mile from the airport. Erickson was still their nearest resemblance to a witness. And now he had to phone Headquarters and start explaining to Buddha Ilford.

"Happy Monday," he said to the hangar at large, and turned away.

CHAPTER THREE

"So you got gutted. Did you expect Ilford to hand you a medal?" asked Phil Moss.

It was late afternoon, he was sprawled back in a spare chair in Colin Thane's office at Millside Division with both feet propped on the battered desk, and that meant Thane's main view was of a pair of down-at-heel shoes and a set of frayed, mud-stained trouser cuffs.

"If that was a medal, he pinned it on a hell of a funny place," admitted Thane sadly.

Moss laughed. But Thane didn't feel amused. When he'd called Headquarters from the airport, Assistant Chief Constable Ilford had made it very plain how he felt. Ilford hadn't lost his temper. He'd gone into a subzero politeness which had almost crackled by the time he'd heard exactly how the Beagle Pup's wreckage had been destroyed.

Then he'd hung up.

"Exactly what did he say?" asked Moss.

"That maybe I'd like a transfer to the Dog Branch—as a dog. If I could pass the tests." Thane leaned across his desk, flicked the intercom switch, and told the orderly at the other end to find some coffee. Closing the switch, he pointed a finger at Moss. "Subject closed. Right?"

"I was being sympathetic," complained Moss. He saw the warning glint in Thane's eyes and gave in. "Mary phoned. Wanted to know how your flu was doing."

"Somebody cares," said Thane. But he was pleased. Mary Thane was the kind of wife who only phoned when she thought it mattered.

"We both reckoned you'd survive," said Moss laconically. "Want to hear how I got on with that checklist?"

Thane nodded.

"No instant miracles," warned Moss. "For a start, the local cop up at Glenfinn is a Sergeant Gordon who sounds like the original Highland bull. But I've put him to work."

A tap on the door stopped him there. It opened, and a young police cadet came in with two mugs of coffee. He handed them one each, then left quickly. Millside's bush telegraph had already passed the word that their divisional C.I.D. chief had been having a bad day.

"What about Francis and the girl?" asked Thane, taking a sip from his mug.

"The post-mortem reports are straightforward, death due to multiple injuries." Moss sniffed his coffee suspiciously then risked a gulp. "The only relative we've got for Anna Harris is an ex-husband in Canada. As far as background is concerned, she's clean—Records say she's not on file."

"Manny Francis?"

"Has family in Edinburgh, who hadn't heard from him in years. He worked as a salesman before he joined Eurobreak—before that he wanted to be a commercial pilot, but couldn't make the grade. Records haven't come back on him yet."

That happened. When things were busy, you took your place in the queue. Thane rose and went over to the grimy window. The sky was beginning to grey outside. On a nearby patch of waste ground some children were playing football with a tin can and in the distance he could see the first neon signs starting to glow as they were switched on above the shops along King Street.

He turned, his eyes straying to the reality of the divisional crime map on the opposite wall and its scatter of incident markers. It was an old map. He'd been promised a new one when Millside got its new police station, which existed as plans and a cleared site. But Strathclyde Region's battered budget had brought the axe down on that and a whole lot of other projects.

"How far have we got with checking on Eurobreak?" he asked, coming back to Moss.

"I've been doing that myself." Moss said it like a guarantee, which it was. "Everything ties with what we were told. John Peebles runs the show, no sleeping partners involved —businesswise, anyway. The travel trade reckon Eurobreak is a bucket-shop discount outfit, but still admit Peebles is doing well." He swung his legs off the desk, levered out of the chair, and added, "Pre-Eurobreak, the word is Peebles ran an advertising agency but too many people didn't pay him their bills."

"It happens." Thane wondered how many hundred times a year it happened in the city. The only casualties heard about were when big firms crashed. "How about his corduroy cavalier, Ellison?"

"Hired help." Moss gave a soft belch and scowled at his emptied coffee mug. "Peter Ellison is married like he said, with a mortgage. What he didn't tell us is he's related to Peebles. But it's reckoned he earns his keep—Peebles comes up with the ideas, Ellison does the legwork." He got rid of the mug by dumping it on a filing cabinet. "I thought your main interest was Manny Francis's pal, Cassill."

"I haven't got a main interest—yet," said Thane. "I'm just trying to keep out of the Dog Branch, remember?"

"Woof," agreed Moss cheerfully. He went over to the door and opened it. "I put Mac on the Cassill angle, and I haven't talked to him yet. But he's outside."

They went out into the main C.I.D. room, which was big and dull, with about a dozen desks, twice as many telephones, and a scatter of lockers and tables. As usual in mid-afternoon, only a few of the desks were occupied by men writing reports or using telephones. In a corner near a window a bulky, middle-aged man in waistcoat and shirt sleeves was tapping determinedly at a typewriter.

They went over to him. Detective Sergeant MacLeod, an irritatingly slow but determinedly thorough individual, kept pecking at the typewriter till he reached the end of a line. Then he looked up.

"Ben Cassill," said Thane. "What have you got?"

"I'm doing a summary now, sir." MacLeod's voice was slightly pained and he laid a hand on the folder beside his typewriter. "It's all here. Southern Division handled him as a fatal accident and—"

"Just the outline, Mac," interrupted Moss, knowing MacLeod's ways. "We'll get the rest later."

MacLeod sucked his lips. "A beat cop found him lying dead in an alley off Tannick Street at two in the morning. That was eight days ago—Cassill had lived on his own up above, on the third floor, his bedroom window was open, the bed had been used, and he was wearing pyjama trousers."

"What did the post-mortem say?" asked Thane.

"Fractured skull and broken neck." MacLeod deliberately flicked over a couple of pages in the folder. "They decided against suicide—it didn't look that way, and there was no note. But Cassill had been on sleeping pills and his doctor was treating him for nervous tension. The way it was put together, a noise outside probably woke him up, he staggered over to the window, opened it—"

"And leaned too far out?" Thane raised a doubting eyebrow. "No flaws?"

"None, except we don't know what wakened him, sir." MacLeod was too old a soldier to go further.

"You get some noisy cats," said Moss. "Any neighbours hear anything?"

MacLeod shook his head. "But I could talk to them."

"Do that," said Thane slowly. "And talk to them about Cassill. If his nerves were jangling, I want to know why."

The plainclothesman who had taken the telephone call was hovering at his elbow with a slip of paper in his hand. He took his chance and gave the note to Thane. One glance at it and Thane cursed softly.

"Phil." He handed the note on.

Records had had Manny Francis on file, with two previous convictions. One dated back a long time and had been a simple assault and theft, with a year's probation.

But the other had been only six years back, when he'd drawn a five-year sentence at Edinburgh High Court for fraud and theft.

"Something else they didn't mention," grunted Moss and calculated to himself. "If he got full remission, he must have walked straight out of prison and started work for Peebles. Would Peebles know?"

"I'm going to find him and ask." Thane glanced at his watch. "Tell the sergeant up at Glenfinn that I'll be there tomorrow—that I'm flying in." He had another thought. "Cassill was a flyer too. Find out if he did much recently and where he went."

"Soak it up and see what we squeeze out." Moss muttered the words under his breath as Thane strode off. His stomach ulcer was nagging again, low-key but an early warning. A few times lately, contrary to everything he'd ever said, he'd even thought of talking to a surgeon. There was a new Health Foods shop down in King Street, and he might look in there instead.

He noticed MacLeod looking at him oddly and gave a grunt.

"Get your backside out of there, Mac," he said. "You've work to do. Think about your pension in your own time."

Sergeant MacLeod refused to be ruffled. He rose ponderously, nodded, and wandered off.

Eurobreak Vacations had its head office located close to the heart of Glasgow's shopping centre, just off Sauchiehall Street.

Colin Thane got there as a department store clock opposite touched 5 P.M. Inside, one of the counter staff led him through the public area to a small elevator hidden behind a screen of potted vines. He went up two floors, emerged in a thickly carpeted executive area, and was met by a good-looking, dark-haired girl who announced she was the managing director's secretary. Giving a dazzling smile, she ushered him into John Peebles' office.

"I didn't expect a visit so soon, but it's good to see you again, Thane," said Peebles, who was in his shirt sleeves. The white-haired boss of Eurobreak was standing in the centre of the big, lavishly furnished room. He dismissed his secretary with a nod and, as the door closed, thumbed towards a cocktail cabinet. "Like a drink?"

"Another time," said Thane, sensing no particular enthusiasm behind the invitation. "This won't take long."

"Good." Peebles grinned, his gold tooth flashing, and glanced at his watch. "I usually vanish out of here before the half hour. Sit down."

Thane took a chair while Peebles returned behind a

large rosewood desk which was absolutely bare except for a carefully centred note pad and a couple of telephones. Despite the prematurely white hair, the man's hard, dark eyes and smooth face suggested he could still be in his late forties.

"Well?" asked Peebles, sitting back and folding his arms. "What's your problem, Chief Inspector? I thought Ellison and I told you all we could this morning."

"I think you left one thing out," said Thane deliberately, and saw Peebles shape a slight, quizzical frown. "Did you know Manny Francis had a record?"

"Yes." The hard, dark eyes met his own unblinkingly. "I knew it when I hired him."

"Then why didn't you tell us?"

Peebles shrugged. "Maybe I nearly did, when I asked why you were so interested in a plane crash. But I reckoned that if it mattered you'd find out on your own."

"Yet you still told Ellison to run an eye over the branch books," reminded Thane pointedly.

"True. They're in order." Peebles lifted a hand and rubbed his chin. "Look, I knew Francis before he landed in trouble, dipping his firm's till to get out of a gambling jam. He came to me, I took a chance, and—all right, at the time I was starting up and I got him cheap. But it paid off, for both of us. Anything wrong in that?"

Thane shook his head.

"Then let me ask you again," said Peebles. "What the hell's worrying your people so much about that crash? Wasn't it an accident?"

"It was an accident, as far as we know," nodded Thane. "Except that ever since, somebody's been very interested in what's left of that plane. Interested enough to come right out in the open today and burn it."

"Your problem, not mine." John Peebles rose to his feet.

"Sorry, Chief Inspector, but my only concern is both Francis and the Harris girl worked for Eurobreak. That part's sweet and clean—"

"And you don't want to get involved." Thane stayed where he was a moment longer. "Ellison passed the message on."

"We'll still help, if we can," said Peebles. "You understand, don't you?"

"Completely," agreed Thane.

He got up and left. The same girl was hovering outside and saw him back to the elevator. She was still smiling.

There was an old Western on television that night and as soon as the evening meal was over in the Thane household the children glued themselves in front of the set.

For once, it suited Thane. He went through to the kitchen and made a pretence of helping Mary stack the dishes. But he spent most of the time just watching her. He liked watching his wife at any time. To be the mother of two school-age children and to be married to a cop seemed load enough for any woman. But Mary, with her long, dark hair, bright eyes, and a figure that still took the same dress size as when they'd married, made a nonsense of it.

In the background, a miniature war began exploding from the television screen in the next room. The rustlers had arrived.

Listening, he grinned then lit a cigarette though he was cutting down his smoking in a big way. He considered Mary again and decided not to tell her yet about the Promotions Board possibility. The whole prospect might be a farce unless things improved, and the chances were being whittled down one by one.

Two reports from Forensic had been waiting for him when he'd called back in at Millside Division after his session with John Peebles. Neither had been particularly helpful.

Nothing had been learned from an examination of the fuel can used to set the Beagle on fire. The Forensic team had also completed their visits to Anna Harris's service flat and Manny Francis's apartment. They'd drawn a blank at the girl's flat. All they'd been able to establish at Francis's apartment was that the scratches around the lock on the opened drawer might be fairly recent in origin. But "might" wasn't a word any court liked hearing.

He drew pensively on his cigarette while the television gunfire raged on. It was the kind of situation where he had reason to be thankful that he had Phil Moss as his number two. Moss had the patience Thane knew he lacked. Moss could be counted on to keep digging away, regardless of the amount of time involved—or how slender a lead he was following.

Right now, all they had was certainly slender enough. Something aboard that aircraft had mattered—mattered enough that if it couldn't be retrieved from the wreckage then it had to be destroyed.

"Colin." Mary had stopped work and was looking at him. "What's wrong?"

"I was thinking. It's a bad habit." He stubbed the cigarette on a dirty saucer, put an arm round her shoulders and took her over to the kitchen window. Outside, it was a clear, moonlit night. He sighed a little. "I've had better Mondays."

"Starting with that flu bug." Mary frowned up at him. "Do you have to make this trip north tomorrow?"

"The way things are, I haven't much option." A thought

struck him. "Remember the Eaglefarm glassware you liked? There might be some kind of link between it and this Glenfinn place."

"That's where it is made," she said patiently. "Didn't you know?"

He blinked. "You're sure?"

"Positive," she said. "They've been in magazine articles. There's some kind of crafts workshop in the village, and that's where they're turned out." She eyed him speculatively. "I still like their stuff."

"I'll keep it in mind," he said. "Bargains or reject seconds—but they'll have to be pocket-money price, believe me."

When she finished tidying they went back through. Tommy, Kate, and the dog were lined in a row in front of the TV set. It was another hour before he firmly shoehorned them off to bed, then, in turn, sat back with a yawn.

"Early night?" suggested Mary.

He agreed. "How about a drink first?"

"You'll get one." Her voice warned him what was coming. "Hot-toddy style—honey, lemon, and whisky. Let's wipe out that flu."

It seemed a waste of good whisky, but he knew better than to argue.

A little later, as he climbed into bed, he set the alarm clock for 7 A.M. That meant a full eight hours' sleep, except he had other thoughts stirring as he lay watching Mary brush her hair at the mirror.

Then the toddy special started to bite, he felt his eyelids closing, he yawned, and five seconds later he was sound asleep.

Glasgow Airport has one of its traffic peaks around 8
A.M. The Glasgow—London shuttle jets are ferrying their
loads of businessmen to morning meetings, Highlands and
Islands flights, Aberdeen "oil boom" traffic and the rest
take their place in the runway queues with the bigger jets
bound for Europe.

But it was quiet over at the light aircraft parking area
when a Millside Division car dropped Colin Thane. He
waved the car on its way again, glanced dubiously at the
grey, overcast sky, then saw Gibby MacDonald waiting for
him at the edge of the tarmac.

"All set?" MacDonald picked up an overnight bag lying
at his feet. "The weather map looks good. Five minutes
will see us clear of this lot."

He led the way out past a scatter of other aircraft to a red
Piper Cherokee which was sitting with its engine idling.
Opening the cockpit door, he tossed the overnight bag into
the rear seat, helped Thane aboard, then scrambled in himself and settled behind the controls.

A power check, a final run over switches and instruments, and the Cherokee started rolling while MacDonald
began a series of radio exchanges with a gravel-voiced controller. They took their place in the runway queue behind a
whining four-engined military transport and watched it go,
then it was the Cherokee's turn.

"Keep that seat-belt fastened," advised MacDonald as
they took off smoothly and the ground shrank below.
"There could be a spot of local turbulence."

The Cherokee shook and dipped as he spoke, then settled as they continued climbing and MacDonald used the
radio again.

"Like traffic lights and halt signs," he said as he finished.

"When you're in controlled air space, you go by the book unless you want a ticket."

Thane nodded, looking down at the city already spread below. "How would it have been when Francis came in?"

"At night?" MacDonald shrugged. "He was making a visual approach, so he'd have the runway lights in sight five minutes out." He pointed to the port wing. "There's the final approach path and the reason he was ordered to gain height. Three high-rise blocks, then the tower cranes at the riverside. If he was low over Fortrose he'd have been a damned sight lower when he reached them."

"The theory is he stalled," said Thane.

"If that's what the department people say then that's how it was," said MacDonald. He ran a hand through his mop of ginger hair and frowned. "Manny Francis was a reasonably good pilot. But I've seen better than him come unstuck—and left sweating blood by the time they got down in one piece."

As MacDonald had promised, the grey cloud was soon left behind. The Cherokee kept on a northerly course and the ground below gave way to sparkling water as they crossed Loch Lomond in bright sunlight. Wooded hills and fields began to give way to the first of the mountains.

"Any notion why Francis flew to Glenfinn so often?" asked Thane, half closing his eyes against the sunlight's glare on the Perspex windshield.

"We're not the absolute backwoods—people do visit and plenty make it a joyride milk run at weekends." MacDonald grinned a little, his hands resting lightly on the controls. "It was bird watching with him—straight, I mean. Little feathered friends, and we've plenty around Glenfinn you don't find easily. He'd hike off from the village with binoculars and a camera."

"Even the last time?"

"He'd a girl with him, hadn't he?" answered Mac-Donald.

The Cherokee buzzed on. The West Highland seacoast town of Oban appeared briefly far to their left then the aircraft's shadow was crossing mountains which still had snow-streaked gullies high on their bare rock sides. It was almost a surprise to Thane when the engine note changed, the flaps operated, and they began to lose height.

Two minutes on, Thane had his first view of Glenfinn. Seen under blue skies from twelve hundred feet, it was a typically straggling Highland village set along a narrow river which snaked through a long, broad glen. The glen was flanked by wooded hills which went on for some distance before the mountains began again, and he caught a glimpse of a line of tall electrical pylon towers.

The airstrip was located about a mile down the glen from the village. As the Cherokee came in, other details began to show. Most of the glen was occupied by a scatter of small farms with cattle grazing in their fields. A main road reached in towards the village from the south, and a smaller road, plus a number of tracks, radiated out again.

Humming to himself, the sound almost lost under the engine's steady purr, Gibby MacDonald brought the plane down to a smooth landing, wheels almost kissing the grass as it taxied in. They stopped close to a hut with a white roof. Nearby were two small hangars and, beside them, a Land-Rover equipped as an emergency tender.

"Home." MacDonald switched off and as the propellor chunked to a halt he gestured towards the hut. "Glenfinn Flying Club—at least the roof doesn't leak."

Leaving the aircraft, MacDonald carrying his overnight bag, they walked towards the hut. One hangar was empty, the other held an aircraft and a partially assembled glider. Thane caught a glimpse of a brightly painted fuel bowser in the background then they reached the hut and, opening the door, MacDonald waved him in.

As they entered a warm, simply furnished clubhouse room, a slim, chestnut-haired girl wearing blue jeans and a red roll-neck sweater came out of a small office.

"You're early, Gibby." She gave MacDonald a welcoming smile which stayed there as her eyes turned towards Thane. "Did you have a good trip, Chief Inspector?"

"He's a prompt passenger and we picked up a tail wind," MacDonald answered for him, heaving the overnight bag into a corner. "This is Lorna Patterson, the boss around here, Chief Inspector. She owns the club—just as important, she'll be flying you back."

"I'm grateful." Thane shook hands with her. Lorna Patterson was in her early twenties, small enough to hardly come up to his shoulders in her flat-heeled slip-on shoes, and had an attractive, pert-nosed face with high cheekbones and a pair of intelligent grey eyes. "What time will suit you?"

"Three o'clock," she suggested. "When Gibby phoned, I'd just booked a flying lesson for one of our local farmers. We'll squeeze you aboard, and he's happy—he hasn't been as far as Glasgow on a lesson before."

MacDonald laughed at Thane's expression. "Relax, man," he declared. "Lorna has full instructor rating and she'll be there to make sure he doesn't get lost."

"Good." Thane glanced round the clubroom. It held a few chairs, a scatter of tables, and an electric fan heater. The nearest thing to decoration was a scarred bulletin board on one wall and there was a small coffee bar. "Any word from your Sergeant Gordon? He was supposed to meet me here."

MacDonald and Lorna Patterson exchanged a glance that was hard to read. Then the girl shook her head.

"He'll be along," she said. "He probably decided to wait until he saw you land. Like some coffee while you're waiting?"

Thane was on his second cup by the time a white Ford police car rolled up and stopped outside the clubhouse.

By then he knew that the chestnut-haired girl had inherited the flying club two years before when her father had died in a road accident and that Gibby MacDonald and an odd-job man amounted to the total staff, with MacDonald on a part-time basis. He spending the rest of his time running a small farm higher up the glen. Lorna Patterson lived with her widowed mother in the village.

"Making money?" asked Thane. As he spoke, he saw a figure in police uniform get out of the Ford and begin walking unhurriedly towards the clubhouse door.

"Enough." The girl looked round for confirmation from Gibby MacDonald, but he had vanished into the tiny office for a moment. "One or two local farmers have their own aircraft and base them here. Then we do some hire work on the side and there are usually a few visiting pilots flying in at weekends."

"Like Manny Francis?"

"Yes." Her smile faded. "That was bad, Chief Inspector. It shouldn't have happened."

"But it did." Thane left it at that as the clubhouse door opened.

The police sergeant who came in was a lean, middle-aged man with a ruddy-hued face and dark, bushy eyebrows. He gave a tight-lipped nod to Lorna Patterson then came over to Thane and gave a careful salute.

"Chief Inspector Thane?" His voice had a soft Highland accent but his manner was cool and neutral. "Sergeant Gordon—"

"You're late," said Thane.

"Sorry." There was no particular regret in the man's voice. "I was delayed, sir. And you were early."

"Then we'll call it even—this time." Thane finished his coffee and got to his feet. "Three o'clock for that lift back?"

The girl nodded. He said good-bye, gave a wave towards Gibby MacDonald, who was just re-entering from the office, and went out to the police car with Sergeant Gordon at his elbow.

"We'll talk in the car," said Thane as they reached it.

Sergeant Gordon's eyes narrowed a little, but he said nothing and they got aboard. Thane waited until the doors were closed.

"What was the delay, Sergeant?" he asked quietly.

Sergeant Gordon shrugged. "One of the farmers up the glen telephoning with a complaint."

"Urgent?"

"Not specially, sir."

"Then next time you're to meet me, be there. Understood?" Thane waited until Sergeant Gordon gave a slow nod, then sat back. "Right, you were ordered to backtrack on what Francis and the Harris girl did here on Sunday. Let's have it."

The man rested his hands on the steering wheel. "They flew in about noon, went over to the Glenfinn Lodge— that's the hotel here—and had a couple of drinks and lunch."

"Then?"

"They left about 3 P.M., hired an old car from a garage, and were seen driving up the Tinker Path—that's a track that leads up into the hills. It's a tourist drive with a wee bit of a loch at the end of it, nothing else. Plenty of visitors go that way."

"Any others that day?"

"Too early in the year." Gordon shook his head. "After that, all I know is they showed up at the flying club about dusk. Francis checked the weather reports, then they drove along to the hotel. They had an evening meal there about nine, left again about eleven-thirty—then it's a blank till they showed up at the landing strip around 1 A.M. They left the car there."

"Did they talk to anyone?" asked Thane.

"A word here and there."

"So you've two blank areas. The time they spent along this Tinker Path, then after they left the hotel at night?"

Sergeant Gordon's ruddy colouring went a shade redder. "That's how it is, sir."

"No, I'll tell you how it is, Sergeant," said Thane. "You're caught up in something a hell of a lot bigger than a four-by-two accident inquiry. So how hard did you try?"

"The best I could." Gordon watched Thane for a moment from under his bushy eyebrows then added, "The way I see it, Francis was probably having it off with the girl at the loch in the afternoon. Then at night—och, he'd had a few drinks at the hotel. Maybe he was just after his money's worth before he took the plane up."

"Sergeant, you've a dirty mind," said Thane. But it could have been that way. He remembered Ilford's advice. Kicking down barricades was one thing, but afterwards the

Strathclyde system had to work. "Maybe you're right. Suppose we ask around again, starting at the hotel?"

Sergeant Gordon hesitated, then gave a slightly sheepish nod.

"Fine." Thane had a sudden thought as the man started the car. "Where's the Eaglefarm Crafts place?"

Gordon looked surprised. "About two miles from here. But I—no, I didn't try there. Is there a reason?"

"My wife likes their glassware," said Thane.

Subdued, Gordon set the police car moving. In a few minutes they were in Glenfinn village, where most of the houses clung along the edge of the single main street.

The Glenfinn Lodge hotel was a white, two-storey structure opposite the village war memorial. Sergeant Gordon was greeted as "Andy" by the hotel staff, but when it came to talking about Manny Francis and Anna Harris they couldn't add to what they'd told before.

The hire-car garage came next. It was a glorified filling station with three pumps and a greasing bay, and the old Morris Mini which Francis had hired was lying in the yard.

"How many miles did he clock up?" Thane asked the garage hand who stood with them.

"First time I've been asked that," said the man with a puzzled glance at Sergeant Gordon. "Andy?"

"You're being asked now," said Gordon.

They got the answer from the garage's hire logbook. The Mini had covered exactly twenty-six miles.

Thane thanked the man and they left. He let the discomfited sergeant trail back with him to the police car and said nothing till they were aboard.

"What's the distance to the loch?" he asked.

"Round trip, about fourteen miles." Gordon looked at him sideways.

"Show me," said Thane.

The loch at the end of the Tinker's Path was too small to have a name. It lay in a hollow of the wooded hills northwest of Glenfinn village and when they reached it after a jolting drive over a dirt road the police car had covered exactly seven miles.

"Anyone live around here?" asked Thane, looking out at the placid stretch of water. Wildfowl were feeding in the shallows and further out a fish surfaced briefly, leaving a widening circle of ripples.

"Not for a long time, sir," said Gordon, shaking his head.

"Then how about him?" asked Thane, thumbing to their left.

A man in heavy tweeds and wearing fishing waders was marching purposefully towards them along the gravel at the edge of the water. He was middle-aged and thick-set, with a broad, bearded face; he had an angler's haversack over one shoulder, and he looked angry.

"I know him," said Gordon in a flat voice. "Captain MacCallum, retired sea captain. Lives in a cottage along the glen, rides a motorcycle like a maniac, and spends most of his time fishing—it gets him away from his wife." He wound down the driver's window as he spoke, then added out of the corner of his mouth, "Ever get the feeling it just isn't your day, sir?"

The tweed-clad angler reached them in another moment, stopped a few feet away, and acknowledged Gordon's greeting with a curt nod.

"Enjoying the fishing, Captain MacCallum?" asked Gordon.

"Like hell I am." MacCallum crunched forward to the car door, ignoring Thane. "Sergeant, this saves me having to come looking for you. It's damned well happened again—"

"Easy," said Gordon. "What's wrong?"

"This." Scowling, the tweed-clad angler dug one hand into his haversack then tossed a plastic bag through the car window into Gordon's lap. Inside the bag was a small, very dead brown trout. "Poisoned—that's what's wrong. The same as last time."

"Here?" Gordon picked up the plastic bag and considered the dead fish with distaste.

"No, the same place as before," snarled Captain Mac-Callum. "The pool on the lower stream—there's a litter of dead fish around it. That's why I came up here, to get some clean fishing."

Gordon sighed. "I'll take a look, captain."

"Four times in six months and you'll take a look? Sergeant, there's a damned poacher murdering fish when he feels like it. If you spent more time finding out what goes on and less driving around admiring the scenery—"

"When did it happen?" asked Gordon, reddening.

"I wouldn't know. I haven't been fishing for a week—my damned fool doctor's orders. But I'm warning you, Sergeant. Do something this time, or you'll regret it."

His glare went from Gordon to Thane. Then he swung on his heel and marched off. Gordon sighed, put the plastic-wrapped fish on the rear seat and shrugged.

"I don't suppose problems like that bother you too much in Glasgow," he said wearily.

"Not often," admitted Thane. "Have you a poacher, like he said?"

"For a kettleful of trout? No, he's ranting about a stream down the glen. Some farmer probably got careless with a chemical spray—or dumped an old drum of fertiliser. But try and tell MacCallum that." He started the car again and blipped the accelerator. "Anyway, he can wait. Where next, sir?"

"The Eaglefarm Crafts place," said Thane. It was almost all that was left on his mental list. "Who runs it?"

"A man called David Harkness and his wife—if you're polite about it." Sergeant Gordon managed a faint smile. "Eve Buchan is her name. They're a strange pair, but they get on well enough with people." He paused, then his curiosity triumphed. "What's your interest, sir?"

"Curiosity," said Thane. "I told you. My wife likes their glass."

It meant a drive back down the winding track, then another three miles along the glen towards a low, hogback hill. An old farmhouse, white with a red roof, was located near the foot of the hill and the start of the lane leading to it had a signpost which took the form of a large copper eagle.

"I'll take this on my own, Sergeant," said Thane as Gordon stopped the car in the cobbled yard. He met the man's surprised gaze quizzically. "What I want you to do is sit and think—think of anything we've maybe missed out on. Right?"

Gordon gave a slow nod. "Thanks for saying 'we,' sir," he said. "I know what you mean."

Thane left the car and walked across the open yard. One wing of the farmhouse had been reconstructed into a showroom and sales area for Eaglefarm Crafts, the rest of it still appeared to be living quarters, and the outbuildings were in use as either workshops or storerooms. A large mongrel dog was sunning itself on the cobbles outside the showroom entrance but ignored him completely.

Pushing open the door, he went into a Highland version of an Aladdin's cave. The walls were hung with deerskin bags, carved wood and knitted sweaters. Glinting in the light, a display case of heavy Celtic jewellery and semi-precious stones sat beside pottery mugs and framed etchings. There were tartan scarves and polished granite desk sets, wooden porridge bowls and finely carved staghorn chess sets—a mixture of qualities and quantities with prices to match.

In the middle of it all the Eaglefarm glassware sat under the beady eyes of a stuffed golden eagle. No two pieces were alike; they took every form and shape from a magnificent leaping salmon to a kilted soldier with rifle and bayonet, and the discreet price tags below them began at around a cop's average wage for a week.

Thane stopped there and was sadly considering a pair of beautifully detailed farm horses, complete with harness and a three-figure cost-price, when he realised someone had joined him.

"Can I help you?" asked a woman's voice.

He turned. She was tall, raw-boned, and in her late forties. Her mousy blond hair straggled out of a leather headband, and she wore a man's red wool shirt tucked into blue jeans which were a size too small around the hips.

"Well?" The woman raised an eyebrow. "You don't look like a customer, not with that police car waiting outside."

"You're right." Thane showed his warrant card.

"A Chief Inspector—that's high rank for Glenfinn." Her voice had a harsh, slightly husky accent which was city rather than country. "I'm Eve Buchan. Wait, will you? I'll get my partner."

She left Thane beside the glassware and was back in a

minute with a thick-set, middle-aged man who wore a dirty leather apron over a wool sweater and khaki army surplus slacks. David Harkness had thinning grey hair and needed a shave. He also had broad, powerful hands but when he spoke his voice was soft and quiet.

"Something wrong, Chief Inspector?" he asked, glancing at the blond woman. "Eve gets the feeling there might be."

"No, I'm looking for help," said Thane. "There was an air accident in Glasgow—"

"Manuel Francis and that girl." Eve Buchan nodded vigorously. "We heard about it."

"Yes." Harkness made a tutting noise with his lips. "We knew them both—as customers, anyway. Is that why you're here?"

Thane nodded. "There are one or two problems about the crash. We're trying to build up a picture of what happened to them that day."

"Then we can't help you," said Eve Buchan flatly. "They didn't come here."

"You're sure?" asked Thane.

"Positive," said Harkness. He tugged an earlobe and smiled apologetically. "Sorry, Chief Inspector—we're open at weekends but at this time of year only Eve and I are around then. We've three of a staff, but they weren't working."

"Then that's it." Thane gestured towards the glassware. "I knew they had some of your work, so I thought I'd check."

"Francis usually looked in when he came up. I think he only brought the girl a couple of times." Harkness frowned for a moment. "We made him a glass aeroplane—special order, and it was a problem. I think the girl got a deer's head."

"It was meant to be a stag," said Eve Buchan dryly, hitching her thumbs in the waistband of her jeans. "Nice people, but that's all we knew about them. People come, people go. I just know what I make and what they buy."

"But not what makes them tick?" suggested Thane.

"Right." She nodded towards the glassware. "Do you know why I like these, Chief Inspector? When I make something in glass I can spot a flaw—anywhere. You can't do that with people."

"I'm not arguing." Thane considered the display. "About people or how you handle glass. These are good."

"That's why they cost," she said. "I'm on glass and jewellery, Dave produces carvings and pottery. The rest"—she looked around and her mouth twisted—"it's mostly just junk we buy in. Tourist bait at pocket-money prices."

"But it's not sold with the Eaglefarm Craft label," said Harkness defensively. "We make that rule."

"I've seen some of your work in stores in town," said Thane. He'd spotted the cheapest item among the glassware, a small, slender vase. A corner of his mind wondered if Mary might like it, then rejected the idea. She wasn't the slender-vase type. "How long have you been based here?"

"Four years. That's when we started—and the place didn't even have a roof on it when we arrived." Harkness gave a brief, reminiscent smile. "Eve and I got together, we both wanted to produce real, worthwhile Scottish craftwork—"

"And if we ever write a book, we'll sell you a copy," said Eve Buchan, cutting her partner short. "I thought you said you had to get back to that kiln?"

"Yes." Harkness looked worried.

"I'm going anyway," Thane told them. "Thanks for your help."

He left the showroom, walked a few paces across the courtyard, then glanced back. They were still standing in the showroom, watching him. Heading on towards the police car, he saw a garage door ajar on the far side of the yard. Inside was a grey BMW coupé, the previous year's model. Eaglefarm Crafts was doing well—on their kinds of prices, they could hardly avoid it.

An hour later he was drinking and eating thick-cut venison sandwiches with Sergeant Gordon in the bar of the Glenfinn Lodge Hotel. Gordon didn't have his cap and wore an old raincoat over his uniform, a signal to the world he was off duty. They had a corner table to themselves and the few other customers were at the other end of the bar, watching a darts match.

"Mind if I ask something, sir?" Gordon took a gulp from his glass, his mood slightly sour again. "Was the trip here really worth it?"

"I left my crystal ball in Glasgow, Sergeant. Right now, I wouldn't know." Thane helped himself to another sandwich and considered the lean, ruddy-faced man with a mixture of irritation and sympathy.

Since they'd left Eaglefarm Crafts they'd talked to the two flying club members who had seen Manny Francis leave on his last flight. All they'd been able to say was as before—that Francis had smelled of liquor but that the aircraft had made a normal, only slightly ragged take-off.

But Sergeant Gordon had lapsed back into a gloomy silence for most of the time, his answers to questions near monosyllabic, his bushy eyebrows framing an occasional, probably unconscious scowl.

"Let's have it, Sergeant," said Thane. "What's your moan?"

"Sir?" Gordon looked at him woodenly.

"You know damned well what I mean." Thane waited.

"It's not you being here." Gordon scowled at his beer.

"I'm relieved," said Thane. "Go on—and that's an order."

"This whole new setup."

"Strathclyde?"

Gordon nodded. "Aye. They want to promote me—"

"So?" Thane gave a surprised smile. "You make it sound like a death sentence."

"Promote me to inspector, and transfer me half across Scotland to some bloody mining town near Glasgow." The man's hands tightened knuckle-white round his glass. "To hell with them—it wouldn't have happened under the old system. I'm a county cop, and this is my kind of country—not your damned coal pits."

"You've got the right to say no and stay here," Thane reminded him softly. "It's in the rules."

"Aye, I know." Gordon shrugged his indifference. "Then they draw an ink line under your name and you stay a sergeant for the rest of your days."

Thane knew what he meant, all too well.

Turn down promotion and the chance didn't come round again quickly—whether you were a cop or a candlestick maker. It was one of the rough edges only time could cure in the Strathclyde setup. New police recruits signed on knowing they could be posted anywhere in the giant region, town, or country. They couldn't refuse and stay in the job.

But serving cops like Gordon, still county men at heart, were different. They could say no, but at a probable cost.

"I've done eight years in Glenfinn," said Gordon. "I run a parish bigger than your whole damned Glasgow with two constables, the nearest of them ten miles from here—them and a handful of civilian 'specials' like Gibby MacDonald—"

"Gibby?" Thane showed his surprise. The young, ginger-haired pilot hadn't as much as hinted at the fact. But in the Highlands the part-time volunteer special constables usually outnumbered regulars.

"Aye. He's mountain rescue squad, like most of them." Gordon took a long swallow at his beer and wiped froth from his lips. "Look, Chief Inspector, I've a wife and kids and I'm not uprooting them. If we were still county, then by now I'd be in line for a local promotion as inspector in this same subdivision." He shook his head. "The way things are now, I'm ready to pack the job in."

That had happened too. Thane rubbed a hand across his chin, thinking of his own already tattered Promotions Board chances. He'd never thought it might mean having to leave Millside Division—or if he had, certainly never thought it might mean leaving Glasgow.

"It's your problem," he admitted. "Change any system to something as different as Strathclyde and a few people are bound to get a rough ride during the first couple of years. That's the way it happens."

"Not with me it won't." Gordon looked out the bar window at the spread of wooded hills. The dark outline of the mountains showed stark beyond. "They can keep their coal pits. As for your Headquarters brass, what would a city man know about the Captain MacCallums who dump dead trout in your lap?"

Thane didn't even try to answer that one.

CHAPTER FOUR

By the time they left the bar there was still about an hour to go before Thane's return flight to Glasgow. Stopping in the sunlit street, Sergeant Gordon sneaked a worried glance at his wristwatch.

"I could give you a lift along to the airstrip now," he suggested. "I'm not trying to get rid of you, sir, but—"

"You've got work waiting. I know," said Thane. "Forget the lift, Sergeant. I'll enjoy the walk. But do me a favour, will you?"

"Sir?" Gordon raised a bushy eyebrow.

"Let me talk to someone about this transfer before you make any more rumbling noises about resigning."

Gordon hesitated. "If you think it can do any good—"

"I didn't say it would," said Thane. "But I can find out."

"Thanks." Gordon took a pace back, saluted, and gave a small grin. "Maybe I'll—well, see you back again, sir."

"I've a feeling you will," agreed Thane and left it at that.

He waited till the sergeant had got back into his car and had driven off. Then he began walking, the sun warming his back and the air smelling sweet. With time to kill, he stopped for a spell at an old stone bridge over a river, just watching the water, then paused again further along to admire the view.

At that kind of pace, it took him half an hour to reach the airstrip. The place was deserted and Thane was standing outside the flying club hut, smoking a cigarette, when a small blue Volkswagen came in off the road and halted near the hut. Lorna Patterson got out of it, gave him a wave, and came over.

"Think we'd forogotten about you?" she asked cheerfully.

"I hadn't got around to worrying," admitted Thane.

"Good." She was still in the same outfit of jeans and sweater and was carrying a leather jacket and a small package wrapped in brown paper. "I—ah—saw Sergeant Gordon down in the village. How did you get on with him?"

"He has his problems," said Thane.

"I know." She led the way into the clubhouse, Thane following her. "Gibby MacDonald told me about this transfer thing."

"Did he?" Thane showed his surprise. The young, red-haired pilot hadn't struck him as having much in common with Gordon.

"They're both in the local mountain rescue team," she explained, going into the office and tossing her jacket and the package on a table. "Sergeant Gordon signed the whole team on as special constables—they get extra equipment grants or something that way."

Thane nodded. He had heard of other mountain rescue teams who had done the same thing. "Special constable" meant being a civilian volunteer, man or woman, who underwent some spare-time basic police training and who was only called out for active duty in emergency situations. They had uniforms at home, their cars were often fitted for police work, and though there were "specials" in the cities, they mattered the most in the country areas, particularly the Highlands, where they outnumbered the regular police in numbers.

"Just how much spare time does Gibby keep for himself?" he asked.

"He manages—most things anyway." Lorna Patterson pinked a little, leaving Thane guessing how some of that spare time was spent. Then she quickly changed the subject. "Was your trip here worth while, Chief Inspector?"

"Hard to say." Thane stubbed the remains of his cigarette in an ashtray. "We gather all the pieces we can. How they'll fit together is something else."

She sighed. "I didn't particularly like Manny Francis. But Anna Harris was pleasant—in fact, I met her in the village that afternoon, just after they'd been at the hotel for lunch."

"Nobody told me that." Thane frowned.

"No reason. We just said hello. Manny Francis had gone to buy cigarettes and she was looking in a shop window."

Thane nodded. "How did she seem?"

"Fine. She told me they were going up to the Eaglefarm place—"

"You're sure?" he asked.

"Yes." She showed her surprise. "Why?"

"Curiosity." Thane played down his reaction. "Did Anna Harris say why they were going?"

"No. Except—I think she mentioned something about Manny Francis wanting a present for someone. I'm not sure."

He didn't press it. But if Francis and the girl had intended going to Eaglefarm Crafts then either something had happened to change that plan or David Harkness and Eve Buchan had lied. And if they had lied—another, unrelated thought crossed his mind.

"Do you keep any kind of log here—who flies in and out, that sort of thing?" he asked.

"Yes. At least, pilot's name and aircraft registration number." Lorna Patterson crossed the little office and came back with a slim ledger. "Here's the current one. Have a look through it if you want." She gestured towards the telephone. "I've a couple of calls to make."

Thane took the ledger out into the clubroom, settled in one of the chairs, and began running a finger down the ink entries. They covered a period of just under a year. Manny Francis's name cropped up for the first time near the bottom of the second page, then at regular intervals. But he was also looking for any other name that might connect. Francis's dead friend Ben Cassill appeared twice as he kept flicking over the pages, then no more.

Suddenly, Thane's finger stopped at another entry and he gave a soft whistle of surprise. The name was John Peebles, the date the previous spring. It didn't have to be the same John Peebles who ran Eurobreak but the coincidence was strong enough to matter, even though Peebles hadn't mentioned being a flyer.

He kept on through the log till he reached the current page. There were no more surprises. Closing it, he went back through to the office. Lorna Patterson wasn't there, and as he laid the logbook on her desk he heard an aircraft engine start outside.

Leaving the club hut, he saw another car was parked beside the blue Volkswagen. Over at the hangar, the Piper Comanche which had brought him north was warming up, and Lorna Patterson stood beside one wing tip talking to a burly young man in farming tweeds.

A moment later he met the learner pilot, whose name was Harry. He had time to return to the club hut, phone

Millside Division, and arrange to be met, then he was stowed in one of the rear seats while Harry was taken through his remaining pre-flight checks. In another few minutes they were airborne, even if Harry's take-off technique was more suited to a plough.

All Colin Thane could do was tighten his seat belt another notch and decide it wouldn't last for ever.

In fact, the rest of the flight went smoothly. Forty minutes later the Comanche made a slightly undignified landing at Glasgow Airport, the red-faced farmer sweating at the controls and Lorna Patterson murmuring encouragement. They taxied off the runway, the plane halted at the light aircraft area, and Thane muttered a hasty thanks and began to climb out.

"Chief Inspector"—Lorna Patterson laid a hand on his arm—"this is yours."

"Mine?" Puzzled, Thane found himself being given the paper-wrapped package he'd seen earlier.

"From Sergeant Gordon," she told him. "He said you'd understand."

Still puzzled, Thane tucked the package under one arm and stepped down on the tarmac. As soon as he was clear, the Comanche's engine increased in power again and it began heading out towards the runway.

Hefting the package suspiciously, Thane walked past the other aircraft. A Millside Division police car was waiting just beyond them and he recognised the big, blond shape of Constable Erickson at the wheel.

"Good trip, sir?" asked Erickson as Thane got into the passenger seat. He didn't wait for an answer. "Inspector Moss couldn't make it. There's trouble with the natives at Fortrose—a code twenty-three."

Thane swore under his breath. Code twenty-three meant group disorder—in plain language, a gang battle.

"Bad?" he asked.

"Seems that way." Erickson gave a half grin. "The division's been ferrying cops out by the vanload for the last half hour."

"Welcome home," said Thane bitterly. He tossed Sergeant Gordon's package into the front shelf. "All right, let's join the party."

The Millside car carved a swift, effortless way through the traffic in the airport area and swooped through the Clyde Tunnel to the north side of the river. Then, while the car radio kept squawking, the tall silhouettes of the Fortrose apartment blocks appeared ahead. In another couple of minutes they reached the heart of the code twenty-three.

Several police cars and an ambulance were drawn up on the edge of a patch of waste ground which held a scatter of old huts and sheds. As Thane's car stopped beside them an unshaven young ned, handcuffed and bleeding from a head wound, was shoved aboard the ambulance by a large, unamused sergeant.

Two other blood-stained woebegone neds were already aboard the ambulance guarded by a young cop who had lost his hat and looked as though most of his temper had gone with it. Other cops, plainclothes and uniformed, were strung out in a thin line along the edge of the huts.

It was a usual enough technique. A second police squad was at work, acting as beaters from the other side of the huts and flushing out any other code twenty-three participants still around.

"Mop-up time," said Erickson, as he and Thane left their car and began heading for the huts.

Thane nodded. They always netted a few thugs when

this kind of clash was broken up. The majority got away after their initial hassle with chains and knives and broken bottles or whatever else they'd had handy. The average cop's view was that as long as no innocent outsider got caught up in it there was no need to weep tears over any thug who was a casualty.

Another ned, wearing jeans and a torn sweat shirt, came into view. Grinning hopefully, hands empty and held well out from his sides, he walked towards the nearest men in the police line. He was grabbed, searched without ceremony, then bundled off towards the cars.

At the same time, Thane heard his name shouted. He turned and saw Phil Moss beckoning from beside another of the scattered huts. He left Erickson, went over, and found his scrawny second-in-command sucking a couple of badly skinned knuckles but looking almost cheerful about it.

"Enjoying yourself?" asked Thane.

"It's a change." Moss wrapped his knuckles in a filthy handkerchief. "Any later and you'd have missed it—the party's over."

"What's it all about?" asked Thane, looking around.

"Anybody's guess." Moss gave a shrug. "The first call said two locals were having a brawl. By the time we got a car out, it was getting like World War III. Uh—and here we go again."

A man was scurrying down a lane between the huts towards them. Behind him, two uniformed men were pounding in pursuit. One of them had breath enough to blow his police whistle as he ran.

"Yours or mine, Colin?" asked Moss.

"Mine. I'm in the mood." Thane took a half step forward, watching the scurrying figure.

The panting ned, a stocky, well-built individual, wore a

quilted jacket which was flapping loose. He had a small firewood hatchet in his right hand and was too intent on running to see Thane ahead of him until almost the last minute. When he did, he tried to swerve to the other side of the lane—and Moss was there, a small, non-regulation black baton in one hand.

Hardly hesitating, the ned changed course again and tried to rush past Thane while he swung the hatchet in a wild, intimidating arc.

Thane sidestepped. But as the man passed he swivelled round on his left heel and kicked with his right. His foot took the man hard on the tail in a way that would have scored a long-range goal on any football field.

It was a kick which literally lifted the ned from the ground. He fell sprawling, howling with pain, the hatchet flying loose—and before he could scramble up again, Moss had retrieved the hatchet and Thane had him in an armlock.

Jerking the ned upright brought another squeal. He made a last frantic effort to get free but Thane countered by propelling him over to the wall of the nearest hut and slamming him hard against it.

"Had enough?" asked Thane.

The ned nodded, and stayed where he was, groaning, while the two uniformed men panted up.

"All yours," said Thane, shoving his captive into their arms. "Any more to come?"

"Don't think so, sir." The older of the two constables took time off from snapping handcuffs on their prisoner and shook his head. "We found this one hiding in a damn garbage pit."

"It probably felt like home," suggested Moss, joining

them. "Well, well"—he grinned—"look who we've got. Soldier Kelly again."

Thane nodded. It was the same "hard man" ex-deserter he'd spotted when he'd been out with Erickson in Fortrose the previous day.

"What's it all about this time, Soldier?" he asked.

Kelly glared at him and used his tongue to wipe at the blood oozing from a split lip.

"I wan' a flamin' lawyer," he managed. "That was plain police brutality—brutality, an' you know it."

"But we're good at it," murmured Moss. He handed the hatchet to one of the constables. "Come on, Soldier. What started this little lot?"

Kelly treated them to a stream of curses. He was still elaborating on the same theme when Thane nodded to the constables and he was dragged off.

"That makes six we've got." Moss stuck his hands in his pockets and glanced around. The police line was breaking up, the men starting back towards their cars. "Looks like it's over—time to go home. How did your trip go, now I've a chance to ask?"

"Hills and grass and cattle," said Thane. "You wouldn't have liked it."

"No." Moss considered the tower blocks around and belched. "Like that song goes, keep me where the ce-ment grows. I know my limitations."

They went back to Erickson and the car and on the drive from there Thane brought him up to date.

The first of the prisoners from the Fortrose street fights were being charged by the bar sergeant when Thane and Moss reached Millside police station. They walked past the public area, with its familiar odour of stale people and fresh disinfectant, headed upstairs to C.I.D. territory, and went straight through to Thane's office.

Dropping down into his battered leather chair, Thane tossed Sergeant Gordon's package on his desk. Then he brought out his cigarettes, counted the number still in the pack, and decided he wasn't doing too badly.

"Like one?" he asked, offering the pack to Moss.

"No, I'll stick with these." Moss produced a pack of his own, which was a surprise.

Then Thane saw the label and winced. They were herbals—he remembered Moss on a previous herbal kick, and that was enough. He gave a warning growl.

"Light one of those in here and I'll heave you through the window," he threatened. "The last lot stunk the place for weeks."

Moss looked hurt but tucked his pack away then watched gloomily while Thane lit one of his own. Then he nodded at the parcel.

"Somebody give you a present?" he asked.

Thane shrugged. He was checking through the list of telephone messages on his desk pad. Two on the list asked him to call Assistant Chief Constable Ilford at Headquarters. The second had the word "Immediate" after it, and was underlined.

"Open it if you want." He reached for the telephone with a sense of foreboding. "The local cop at Glenfinn sent it—it could be a bomb, the way he feels about life."

He watched Moss unwrap the package while he put a call through to Buddha Ilford. Then he heard Moss chuckle at the same moment as Ilford's brusque voice sounded over the line.

"You got back," said Ilford.

"Yes, sir. Then we had some trouble out at Fortrose—" out of the corner of his eye he saw Moss holding up a plastic-wrapped bundle consisting of one dead fish and a small bottle.

"Tell me another time," rasped Ilford. "I've a Man-power Committee meeting in a couple of minutes. Thane, who authorised you to go hiring aircraft?"

"I didn't, sir. I was offered the ride, no charge." Thane grimaced at Moss, who was still holding the dead fish.

"Well, tell me what you're doing next time." Ilford broke off and Thane heard him coughing over the line. The Headquarters brand of flu germ was still in business. After a moment, Ilford began again, less irate. "Was it worth while?"

"Maybe. I'm not sure yet," answered Thane.

"Meaning you don't know," said Ilford. "Another thing —I hear you're unhappy about somebody called Cassill who fell from a window."

"Interested in him," corrected Thane. He slipped his hand over the mouthpiece and glanced at Moss. "Cassill, Phil—anything?"

Moss nodded. "Tell him it's shaping."

Uncovering the mouthpiece, Thane did.

"Good," was Ilford's curt comment. "Add this to your list—presuming you've got one. Inland Revenue are interested in the whole Eurobreak operation. I had a couple of their top vultures round this morning wanting to pick over anything we collect from the Manny Francis business."

"Who told them there was a Manny Francis business?" asked Thane.

"Computer gossip," said Ilford gloomily and broke off for another brief coughing session. "It's my fault. I asked our Command computer to ask the Revenue unit if Manny Francis was a name that meant anything. It was a hunch— but it wasn't Francis that interested their computer, it was the fact he worked for Eurobreak."

"What's their interest?" Thane frowned at the mouth-piece, wondering what was coming next.

"The way Eurobreak keeps growing when their tax re-turns show the firm is hardly breaking even. The company books seem cast iron, but the Revenue mob smell some-thing wrong." Ilford gave a sigh. "Look, you'd better come round first thing tomorrow. This whole damned business is getting out of hand."

The distant receiver went down before Thane could reply. He gave a soft curse, hung up his own phone, and found Moss waiting resignedly.

"Now the tax men are getting in on the act." Thane told him the rest then scowled down at the opened parcel on his desk. "What does Sergeant Gordon expect me to do with this lot?"

"Lab. tests," said Moss. "Seems you promised him all Strathclyde's facilities were always on tap. There's a note from him."

"Great," said Thane sarcastically. "So he uses me as a messenger boy."

"You must have sold him quite a line," said Moss. "Hooked his interest, you could say." ·

"Go to hell," said Thane. He shoved the package to one side. "Tell me what we've got on Cassill's death—and it better be good."

Moss nodded, ambled across the room, opened the door, and gave a shout. The summons brought Sergeant Mac-Leod who came in and stood like a bulky statue, waiting his cue.

"Ben Cassill," said Moss. "Tell it again, Mac."

"I asked around his neighbours and that sort of thing like you wanted, sir." MacLeod fished a notebook from one pocket but didn't bother to open it. "I found a couple who heard a car driving away from the lane not long before he was found dead. They remember, because it had a noisy exhaust."

"That wasn't in the original reports." Thane gave a glance towards Moss, who shook his head in agreement.

"They didn't bother mentioning it last time," said Mac-Leod gloomily. "Everybody seems to have decided it was an accident from the word go." He paused for effect. "Then there's a story about a row between Cassill and someone else—that was a week or so earlier."

"Well?" Thane kept his patience with an effort. "Do we get to hear about it?"

"Sir." MacLeod nodded seriously. "Another neighbour—the woman who lives above Cassill's flat." He gave a heavy-shouldered shrug. "She was away from home for a week when Cassill was killed. The divisional man didn't get to see her."

Thane said nothing. But he had an idea the divisional man concerned had trouble coming, and soon. He nodded for MacLeod to go on.

"Seems she came home late from a bingo session, sir. Cassill's door was open and he was having a real row with another man. When Cassill saw her, he banged the door shut—she didn't see the other character and didn't catch what the quarrel was about." MacLeod paused, flicked his notebook open for a moment, then closed it again, savouring the final titbit. "But she did hear a car drive off soon afterwards. And it had a noisy exhaust too."

"Nicely done, Mac," said Thane. "Anything else?"

MacLeod shook his head.

"Right. Write it up, formal statements." Thane remembered the parcel in front of him. "Take this out with you—make sure it gets to Forensic at Headquarters."

Solemnly, MacLeod gathered up the dead fish, the little bottle of water, and their wrappings and went out.

"Back to the old routine," said Moss as the door closed. "Did he fall or was he pushed—and I know which way I'd bet."

"Cassill was on tranquilizers." Thane eased back in his chair and considered the ceiling for a moment. "That was new. So we'll say something was worrying him sick. What else?"

"Manny Francis sent him a wreath." Moss scratched his shirt front vigorously. "Friendly—but that's the lot in that direction. Still, remember how that corduroy kid Ellison told us he'd never heard of Cassill?"

Thane nodded.

"He's lying. I went round to Cassill's office and they'd kept his desk diary. Ellison's name is on his contact list, with the Eurobreak head office number." Moss grinned like a hungry shark. "You didn't get anywhere with his boss—Peebles didn't even mention he was a flyer. But his right-hand man, little friend Ellison, might be easier."

"Maybe." Thane thought about it. "We'll try it. But we'll let him get home tonight first."

It often worked better that way. Most people had their guard down in their home environment, found it harder to lie—particularly if there was an anxious relative floating around just out of earshot.

He looked round as there was a knock on the door. It opened, and a young, fresh-faced detective strode in. Detective Constable Beech was known for two particular reasons. He fell in and out of trouble with monotonous regularity, and he was the only cop in the division who was the father of twins. Neither situation ever seemed to worry him.

"The Fortrose caper, sir," he said breezily. "I've got the final score. We've booked four downstairs and they're in the cells. There are another two due in once they've been patched at hospital, and we've one uniformed cop with a couple of cracked ribs."

"Find out what it was about yet?" asked Moss from the side.

"They've gone dumb, as usual," shrugged Beech, then switched his attention to Thane again. "What about Soldier Kelly, sir? He's booked on a holding charge, like the rest. But he had a go at you with that axe—we could take it to attempted murder."

"All I saw was a warning gesture," said Thane. "Forget it, Beech. Save the taxpayers' money. Did you check through what they had on them?"

Beech nodded. That was standard procedure when a bucketload of neds was brought in. Time after time, items from their emptied pockets had linked them with other cases in the divisional books.

"They were clean, sir." He grinned. "Except for Soldier Kelly—would you believe he's applying for a passport?"

"I met his wife once," said Moss. "They deserve each other—no wonder he wants a passport. I'd have skipped from her long ago."

Thane frowned. "I thought you said they weren't talkative."

"He'd the Passport Office application form in a pocket," explained Beech. "He made a noise about going abroad for a holiday."

"The trouble is, we'll have to let him back in again," said Thane. "Anything else?"

Beech shook his head and left them in peace again. They talked around the whole situation for another spell, getting nowhere. When Phil Moss finally went out, he had a few things to be added to the checklists, from a C.R.O. scan on the couple who ran Eaglefarm Crafts to a try at tracing whether John Peebles had received his pilot training with the Royal Air Force—and if he had, what his service record had been like.

It left Thane with a chance to look through the paperwork which had accumulated on his desk. He signed some expense sheets and mileage claim forms, fed the usual circulars from IN to OUT tray, then took a break. Lighting another cigarette from his self-imposed ration for the day, he lifted the telephone and dialled his home number.

A barely recognisable croak came from the other end of the line when the call was answered.

"I've got your damned flu," managed Mary Thane with an effort. "When are you coming home?"

"Late," said Thane. "That's why I called."

She gave a cross between a wail and a groan. "Then I'll feed the kids when they get home and take to bed—if I last that long."

"Try aspirin," suggested Thane.

"Like hell." She attempted a rude noise. "This once, I'll belt the cooking sherry. So don't waken me, comrade."

He grinned, said good-bye, hung up, and tackled the next handful from the IN tray.

It was dark by seven and a drizzle of rain began about half an hour later, leaving the streets glinting under the lights. It was still drizzling when the duty car took Thane and Moss out to Peter Ellison's house, and they passed two road accidents in the first mile, both of them wet-weather skid collisions with the drivers arguing over the damage.

Moss had been on his herbal cigarettes. The odour clung to his clothing and Thane saw the duty driver, a late-shift man, sniffing and looking puzzled as he steered through the traffic. Farther out, a truck had left the road on a bend and gone through a wall. Two beat cops and an ambulance were already there, and Thane remembered what it had been like to be in uniform and out on a night when the rain ran down the back of your neck.

The herbal odour still rankled. He lit one of his own cigarettes in reluctant self-defence and had just finished it when they reached their destination.

Peter Ellison lived in a small, fairly new housing estate on the northwest side of town, the kind where every couple had a king-sized mortgage but pretended they'd bought outright and where two cars and a daily household help were the accepted norms. The Eurobreak account executive's home was a ranch-style bungalow with a large garden on a corner site.

Thane and Moss left their driver on radio watch at the gate, walked up a slabbed path to the front porch of the house, and rang the doorbell. A hall light came on, the door opened, and a young, pretty brunette wearing an apron over a blouse and skirt smiled out at them.

"Yes?" she asked.

"Police, Mrs. Ellison." Thane gave her an easy smile in return. "Is your husband at home?"

"Yes." She looked surprised. They usually did. "But—"

"He's been helping us," said Moss smoothly. "The plane crash—"

"Manny Francis and that girl?" She relaxed and nodded.

"He told me. You'll find him round the back, in our garage. He's fixing something on his car."

They thanked her, then, as she closed the door, they walked round the shadowed garden to the rear of the house. A large two-car garage lay open, lights blazing inside and occupied by an elderly white Mini and a sleek blue Lancia coupé. The rear of the Lancia had been raised on a pair of metal ramp-stands and a pair of feet protruded from underneath it.

"Busy down there?" asked Thane loudly as they reached the feet.

The result was a clatter of tools and a startled exclamation. Then Peter Ellison wriggled out into view and stared up at them in surprise for a moment before his pock-marked face switched to a quick smile and he scrambled to his feet.

"I didn't expect visitors," he said apologetically, using one hand to comb back his long, dark hair. He was in old clothes and his hands were grimy. "If you'd come earlier I could have used some help—I'm no car mechanic."

"What's the trouble?" asked Moss.

Ellison shrugged. "The exhaust system—it's holed, and the thing has been making a noise like a train. I bottomed the car hard a few weeks back, holed it, and it's been getting worse ever since."

"Sounds like a replacement job," said Thane, hiding his reaction to the calm statement and keeping his voice casually level. "Expensive, though."

"Right. But the trouble is the agents don't have a replacement in stock. They've had to order—so I've been bandaging the hole, temporary style." Ellison walked over to the garage workbench, wiped his hands on a rag, and turned to face them again. "Well? Is this when I ask if you were just passing the door?"

"It's no social call." Thane went over and joined him at the workbench, his manner still deliberately casual but a new edge to his voice. "You lied to us, Mr. Ellison. It may not be important, but we'd like to know why."

"Say again?" Ellison's pockmarked face flushed. "Now, look—"

"Of course, it could be you just made a mistake," suggested Moss laconically. "People can forget—sometimes."

His mouth a tight line, Ellison looked at them in turn. "What did I forget?"

Thane shrugged. "Well, you told us you'd never heard of a man called Ben Cassill."

"I see." Ellison frowned at his feet.

"Yet Cassill had your name and telephone number on his private list," said Moss helpfully. "Like to explain?"

This time, Ellison visibly winced. "I—all right, I did know him. But I've been told by John Peebles that we've to keep Eurobreak's name out of anything that's going on —and he's the boss."

"Peebles told you to say you didn't know Cassill?" asked Thane.

"No, not specifically." Ellison shook his head nervously, then turned away, making a show of tidying some of the tools on the workbench. "Anyway, I only met Cassill a few times, when he came round trying to sell his pencils and notepads."

"He fell out of a window," reminded Thane.

"So?"

"So we're wondering if maybe you lied about anything else," said Moss bluntly.

"Like what?" Ellison swung round, his face twitching. He had a narrow, sharp-tipped screwdriver in one hand and jabbed it towards Thane's face like an angry pointer. "What are you two damned well getting at?"

"Easy." Thane grabbed the man's wrist, twisted, and made him drop the screwdriver in one quick, fluid movement which brought a gasp of pain from Ellison. "You wouldn't like to see anyone injured by a thing like that, would you, Mr. Ellison?" He let go and stood back. "Anything else you forgot, now you've had a chance to think?"

"No." Still nursing his wrist, Ellison scowled.

"Maybe we should talk to your wife instead," said Moss, and a new look of fear built on Ellison's face.

"Not this time, but maybe next," said Thane curtly.

He turned and walked out of the garage while Ellison was still trying to mutter a reply. Moss was at his heels, and they didn't look back until they were inside the Millside car again.

"You cut that short enough," said Moss, puzzled. "We were just beginning to scare the hell out of him."

Thane nodded. That was all he wanted at that moment.

"And the silencer, the noisy car—" began Moss again.

"I want to see what he does," answered Thane. "We'll give him a little rope, Phil. But it means having a good man on his tail. Who's handy?"

Moss thought. "Young Beech—but he'll be on overtime."

"And he can use the money," said Thane. "Get him."

A nod to their driver set the car moving. They stopped out of sight, round the next corner, and Thane waited while Moss used the car radio. The amount of overtime worked by every cop in the city kept climbing. But the force was undermanned, always had been, and one of the latest temporary economy measures had been a complete halt to recruiting. Politicians didn't seem to care how thin the overtime cover by cops like Beech was stretched as long as they kept the voters happy.

Moss took a couple of minutes to relay the instruction and obtain an acknowledgement. When he put the microphone down, his stomach chose that moment to give a noisy rumble.

"Even a cop is supposed to eat regularly," he complained.

"All right," agreed Thane. "I'm eating at home. You can share if you wash up."

"With you cooking?" Moss grimaced then nodded. "I'll risk it. But don't expect compliments."

The Millside car dropped them at Thane's home twenty minutes later, then drove away, the driver going off duty. The house was in darkness as Thane opened the front door and he switched on the hall light, then left Moss there while he tiptoed upstairs.

The two children were asleep in their rooms, faces like miniature angels. Kate had a doll tucked in beside her.

He went on to the other bedroom. Mary was asleep too, with the soft glow of a bedlight shining beside her and an abandoned paperback lying on the floor. An empty sherry bottle was on his pillow with a note against it which said quite simply "Go to hell. Love, Mary."

He grinned and very quietly switched off the bedlight. Then he went back down to join Moss, who had gone through to the kitchen where Clyde had got out of his dog basket and was alternately yawning and wagging his short stub of boxer tail.

It didn't take long to organise coffee, toast, and a giant-sized cheese omelette. Moss checked in by telephone with Millside while the omelette was being made, then they ate hungrily. Afterwards, once the kitchen was squared up, they settled down again at the kitchen table with a bottle of whisky, two glasses and a jug of water in front of them, and Clyde curled up at Thane's feet.

"I've been thinking," said Moss suddenly.

"Congratulations." Thane waited.

"About where all this is going." Moss nursed his drink. "We haven't the slightest damned idea, have we?"

"Not yet," admitted Thane.

Apart from seeing Ellison, they had the result of the Eaglefarm Crafts checkout. It was fairly negative. The BMW car he'd seen in the farmyard was registered, according to central Vehicle Owners' Index, in the name of Eve Buchan. Neither she nor David Harkness had any known police record and only a few wisps of background had been gathered by tapping the cuttings library in a newspaper where the editor was friendly and kept his mouth shut.

The woman had graduated through Glasgow School of Art. Graduated with merit, though she'd spent more time being a student Communist than at classes. Her political phase hadn't lasted long after that, and she'd built a reasonable reputation in art circles even before she'd gone into partnership with Harkness in founding Eaglefarm.

Even less was known about Harkness. He'd started as an apprentice printer, then drifted through various jobs in the industry. The nearest he'd got to formal art studies had been some night-school sessions, and the rest, according to the critics, was natural talent.

"Peebles," said Moss, as if reading his thoughts. "Not much there either."

Someone at the Ministry of Defence records section had worked fast. The teleprinter answer to their query about John Peebles had said he'd served as an RAF sergeant pilot, mostly on piston-engined transports. He'd come out with a good record and a clean discharge, and that had been twelve years ago.

"That's why Ellison matters, and not just for Cassill's death," said Thane softly. "He's our toehold."

"Uh-huh." Moss lifted the bottle and carefully half-filled his glass again. "Heard this buzz from Headquarters that there's a Promotions Board coming up?"

Thane kept a wooden face at the sudden switch. "So?"

"You. Heard anything?"

"A hint," admitted Thane. "I've to keep my nose clean. Why?"

"This." Moss patted his thin stomach. "If you make superintendent, they'll probably move you. If that happens, I might get my ulcer hauled out—hospital style, a cut and welding job." He looked miserable at the prospect. "At least, I'm thinking about it."

"Why wait?" asked Thane.

Moss scowled. "Why rush?"

The telephone ringing in the hall ended it there. Thane went through and answered it. When he came back, he nodded at Moss's drink.

"Finish it. Beech called in. He says Ellison left home half an hour ago and has just arrived at John Peebles's place." He corked the whisky bottle as he spoke. "Control says there's another reason he wants us out, but he wouldn't explain why."

He left Moss and went upstairs. Mary was stirring and half awake, as he'd expected. Telephones always wakened her. She made a murmuring noise as he bent over and kissed her. Then he went back down.

Two minutes later he was at the wheel of his old Hillman station wagon with Moss in the passenger seat and they were on their way.

CHAPTER FIVE

John Peebles lived south of the river, out beyond the Glasgow city boundary, in a prestige area where the suburbs had faded and a king's mini-ransom could buy a one-time farmhouse or luxury converted cottage. It was the kind of area where the liquor store delivered once a week and was paid promptly once a month and privacy meant you could stand at the front door in the morning and not see a sign of your nearest neighbour.

Following the directions he'd been given, Colin Thane drove along a dark, winding country road until a car's lights blinked twice on ahead. A few seconds later he pulled off the road onto a hard shoulder of ground and stopped his station wagon beside Detective Constable Beech's small, battered two-door Ford. Switching off engine and lights, he got out as Beech came over through the thin drizzle of rain.

"I took a chance it was you, sir." Beech gave him a wary grin. "I'm hoping you'll find this interesting."

"We'd better," said Moss, turning up his coat collar as he joined them. "What's all the damned mystery?"

"It's more a guess than anything." Beech thumbed towards the stretch of woodland which began a few yards from the road. "The house is over that way. We can leave the cars here—they won't be spotted."

They set off, through a mixture of wet grass, mud, and

occasional snapping twigs. Beech led the way and finally stopped them as the trees began to thin again.

"Over there, sir," he told Thane, his young face a mere silhouette in the darkness.

On ahead, lights glowed from a small, modernised cottage. It had white walls and a high, tiled roof. The scent of woodsmoke wafted in the air from one of the chimneys.

"I checked it was Peebles's place," said Beech. "Then— well, what matters is round the front."

They followed him again, Moss cursing under his breath as low scrub clawed at their legs. This time, Beech took a curving route which clung to the edge of the trees, and when they stopped they were looking directly at the front of the cottage and the driveway which led to it from the road. Three cars were parked on a gravelled courtyard, all close under the bright glow of light spilling from the front porch.

Thane gave a thin whistle of surprise. Ellison's Lancia was there, beside a white Jaguar sports saloon he hadn't seen before. But the third car was the grey BMW from Eaglefarm Crafts.

"I asked Control for a registration make on the other two cars," said Beech softly. "The Jaguar belongs to Peebles. But they said you'd already had a check on the BMW this afternoon—I thought maybe it mattered."

"It does." Thane didn't elaborate. "When did it arrive?"

"Before Ellison did—that's all I know." Beech sounded almost apologetic. "I haven't seen anyone moving around since I got here."

"All right, let me guess." A low sigh of resignation came from Moss, who was just behind them. "We wait."

They did, sheltering under the trees for over an hour while the light drizzle continued. Then as Moss complained for the twentieth time that his feet were cold the cottage door suddenly opened. Three people came out into the brightly lit porch.

The man in the middle was John Peebles, his erect figure and white hair instantly identifiable. The others, wearing coats and obviously departing, were Eve Buchan and her stockily built partner, David Harkness. After a moment on the porch they moved across to the BMW and stood beside it, talking earnestly.

At last, the tall blonde got into the driving seat and Harkness climbed in on the passenger side. The car moved off, headlamps raking the night as it made a tight, crunching turn on the gravelled yard. John Peebles went back to the porch, stood there until the car had vanished down the driveway, then went back into the cottage and closed the door.

"Seen enough?" asked Moss hopefully. "Look, my feet—"

"Are cold. We've heard." Thane felt strangely undecided without knowing why. They had tied in the Eaglecraft couple to John Peebles—which meant to Ellison as well. The long car drive down from Glenfinn wasn't the kind of journey anyone took without solid reason, and if they were heading back there now it would be long after midnight before the BMW reached home. He chewed his lip for a moment, glad that the darkness partly hid his indecision. "No, we'll wait again, Phil. Ellison's still in there."

That took another half hour under the trees, while the drizzle died and pale moonlight filtered through the broken cloud overhead. An owl began an occasional soft hooting, and twice they heard a sudden scurry of movement that ended in a small animal's death cry as some unseen hunter struck with claws or teeth.

At last the cottage door opened again and Peebles came out with Ellison. They walked together to Ellison's car, Peebles slapped Ellison cheerfully on the back, and a moment later Ellison got aboard.

"Beech." Thane glanced round at the younger man. "Get back to your own car. If he goes home, call it a night. Otherwise, stay with him."

Beech hurried away. Over in the courtyard, Ellison started his car but talked with Peebles for a little longer with the car door open and the engine idling. Then Peebles said a loud good night, the car door closed, and Ellison drove away. This time Peebles walked straight back into the cottage and the porch light went out a matter of seconds after the door had closed.

"Now can we go home?" pleaded Moss.

Thane nodded and they started back through the trees. Putting a tail on Ellison had paid off in a way he hadn't really expected. He glanced at Moss, plodding along at his side. So far, they'd uncovered a possible murder and a whole series of lies and evasions. But what else was to come? They needed a solid peg of fact before all the rest could be hung together in any kind of shape.

Reaching the car, he got aboard and sat silent for a moment, still thinking. Moss got into the passenger seat, closed his door, and began making impatient noises.

"Finished," said Thane.

He set the Hillman moving, dropped Moss off at his boardinghouse on the way back through town, then from sheer habit looked in at the Millside Division office.

Things were relatively quiet. There had been a stabbing at the far end of King Street, some teen-age vandals had been caught wrecking cars in a parking lot, and two men had been hauled down from a church roof, where they'd been stripping lead for its scrap value. That left the usual assaults and break-ins, including one at a leather-goods store where the manager, working late, had been surprised and left gagged and bound.

Thane went home after that. The house was in darkness as before and this time even the dog didn't bother to greet him. He made himself a mug of coffee, listened to the late-night radio news, and got to bed about midnight.

The bedside alarm wakened him at 7 A.M. Mary was still asleep and he got up quietly, shaved and dressed, and was thinking about wakening the children when the telephone began ringing. He got to the phone in the hall at the same time as Mary's sleepy voice answered on the bedside extension.

The duty sergeant at Millside Division was on the other end of the line.

"You're interested in a man called Ellison, sir," he said as Mary hung up.

"Right," said Thane. "Why?"

"Well"—the sergeant hesitated—"Headquarters Control thought we'd better know. He's dead. His wife found him this morning."

Thane swore in sheer disbelief, his grip tightening on the receiver.

"What happened?" he demanded.

"Accident or suicide, sir." The sergeant's voice made it plain he didn't particularly care. "He was in his garage, that's all I know. The local cops are out there now."

"Tell them I'm coming out," said Thane bitterly. "Send a car round for me, then get hold of Detective Constable Beech and get him out there too."

He hung up and swore under his breath again, his mind still struggling to accept the news.

"Trouble?" asked Mary behind him. She was in her dressing gown and still yawning.

"Trouble," he said. "How do you feel?"

"Like the original flu germ." She saw his expression and gave a quick frown. "No, I'll be all right. When do you have to go?"

Thane had time to gulp a cup of coffee and smoke his way through a cigarette before the C.I.D. duty car, Erickson at the wheel, drew up outside.

Twenty minutes later he arrived at Peter Ellison's house.

Three police cars and one of the white Land-Rovers used by Forensic were parked outside the ranchhouse-style bungalow in the bright morning sunlight. A uniformed constable was stationed at the driveway entrance which led round to the garage at the rear of the neatly kept garden and Thane caught a glimpse of a policewoman standing behind one of the house windows.

He returned the constable's salute with a nod, walked round to the garage, and found the doors open. Ellison's Lancia and his wife's Mini were both in the garage, and four Northern Division C.I.D. men were grouped round the rear of the Lancia. One of the Northern men, a lanky, laconic inspector named Walker, left the others and greeted him with a nod.

"Grand day," said Walker sardonically. He jerked his head towards the car. "The word I got was that this one mattered to you."

"The word was right." Thane pursed his lips. He'd worked with Walker before, and found him reasonable. "How far have you got?"

"Basics. I've talked to his wife, but I took it easy. He's still under the car, where she found him—Doc Williams and Matt Amos are in back, making mumbling noises. You can see the rest for yourself."

"What's his wife's story?" asked Thane. Inwardly, he felt a sense of partial relief. To have the city's senior police surgeon and the Forensic Laboratory's assistant director out with the team meant someone at Headquarters had sense and had been punching the right buttons.

"Like I said, I didn't push her," said Walker. "She's young, she's—hell, I suppose the word is nice. Right now, she's shattered."

"She isn't alone," said Thane. "Go on."

"Right." Walker stuck his hands in his pockets and frowned at the sky, concentrating. "For a start, she says the police were here last night. You?"

Thane nodded.

"About an hour after you left, Ellison told her he had to go round to his boss's house to talk business. He said he'd be late and she wasn't to wait up. She didn't—went to bed about ten-thirty then half wakened sometime later and thought she heard his car going into the garage. But he didn't come in straightaway and she went back to sleep."

"Let me guess," said Thane. "Ellison was working on the car earlier."

"Right, and she thought he was finishing the job," agreed Walker. "Except his side of the bed was empty this morning. So she ran out to the garage in a panic, opened the doors and—well, found him."

"I'll talk to her later." Thane glanced round at the scene in the garage, anxious to get there but with a necessary protocol to sort out. "Ellison was part of something I'm working on."

"No sweat," said Walker, with an understanding grin. "We'll do the usual divisional legwork, but he's yours."

Thane left him and went into the garage. The sour odour of stale exhaust fumes was still heavy in the air as he eased past the other C.I.D. men and reached the rear of the Lancia. Doc Williams and Matt Amos were both there, the police surgeon in his usual immaculate pin-stripe suit, the Forensic assistant director in a leather jacket and slacks. They were lying side by side on the gritty concrete floor and arguing quietly as they peered at the underside of the car and what lay beneath it.

"Move over," said Thane in a flat voice, getting down beside them.

Doc Williams obliged. Nodding a welcome, Matt Amos swung the battery lamp he was holding so that it played on the dead man whose feet protruded between them.

Peter Ellison had died on his back under the car's exhaust pipe, his head and shoulders under the silencer box with only inches of clearance.

Apart from the strange cherry-red hue of his face and the way his mouth hung open with what could have been flecks of dried foam at the corners, he might have been sleeping. His legs were slightly drawn up, his left arm had fallen across his chest, and his half-opened right hand still loosely clutched a small screwdriver.

"Looks easy enough to read, doesn't it?" said Amos, his bearded face an unemotional mask. The beam of the battery lamp shifted to the silencer box and the glass fibre strip bandaged round it, secured by retaining clips. "A do-it-yourself repair job that wasn't quite right—then he crawls underneath with the engine running to tighten things up. Damn stupid, but it happens. Except"—he paused and glanced at Thane—"in this case, maybe that's too obvious?"

Thane stayed silent. The way Ellison lay was the easiest

position for a man to get at the silencer box. Though the dead man was wearing his corduroy suit, he was lying on a rumpled strip of old canvas as if it had been put down to prevent his clothes being soiled by the garage floor.

"Finished?" Amos switched off the battery lamp without waiting for an answer and they got to their feet, joining Doc Williams. The latter was carefully cleaning his hands on a piece of waste rag. Putting down the lamp, Amos eyed Thane with a quizzical sympathy. "How much did he matter, Colin?"

"Enough. We tailed him most of last night—till he got home." Thane switched his attention to the police surgeon. "What can you tell me so far, Doc?"

"Very little." Doc Williams had a habit of brutal honesty. He was slim, dark-haired, and always well-dressed. For the moment, his immaculate appearance was spoiled by a smudge across his nose which had to have come from the underside of the car. "Once I get him out of here it should be different but"—with a faint irritation he glanced at Amos—"at the moment, I'm last in the queue."

"Five minutes more," promised Amos, unperturbed. "Then you can have him. We've got our photographs and most of the rest. All we need are a few measurements."

"Let's hope you remembered your ruler this time," said Doc Williams. Then he switched to a brisk, businesslike manner. "Apparent cause of death is carbon monoxide poisoning, Colin. The colour of his face would spell that out to a first-year student." He gestured at their surroundings. "With the doors closed and a car engine running the atmosphere in here would be lethal in about five minutes— say six to be sure."

"Time of death?" asked Thane.

Doc Williams frowned. "Around midnight. Or a little

earlier—a cold garage floor isn't the ideal place to find a body. It plays hell with your arithmetic in terms of body temperatures."

"You tell us something, Colin." Matt Amos had unwrapped a stick of gum. He put it in his bearded mouth and began chewing. "How new was that bandage round the silencer box?"

"He was fitting it when we were here last night—or that's what he told us."

"It looks that way," Amos said. "There is some road dirt on it, but disturbed here and there—he could have been adjusting it." He kept chewing for a moment, puzzled about something else. "Doc, wouldn't you have expected him to try to get out of there? Wouldn't he have felt dizzy or something first?"

"That can happen, but not too often." Doc Williams chose his words carefully. "Carbon monoxide doesn't have colour or odour—it doesn't even irritate the senses. It's—well, a stealthy killer. Usually the victim just gradually feels dull and drowsy, then passes out."

Despite Amos's question, he and Thane both knew what Doc Williams meant. Carbon monoxide was an insidious killer, all the more dangerous because it could come from so many different sources.

Exhaust gas from cars was just one of them. Town gas, smouldering waste heaps, bathroom water heaters, even explosions in confined spaces could all produce it in poisonous quantity. When people died in a burning building the cause of their death, in most cases, was the carbon monoxide quantity in the smoke. Even the ones who were saved and recovered from the gas could suffer nervous or mental damage.

Under the Lancia, working in the confined space of the

garage, Ellison might never have known the rapid way death was creeping up on him. People did stupid things, he might well have thought he had plenty of safety margin.

Except Thane couldn't believe it. Not after the way he and Moss had pressured the man and not after the meeting they'd seen taking place.

"Know something?" asked Amos softly. "It's too neat, Colin." He glanced at Doc Williams for support. "This one gets the full treatment."

Williams nodded then cleared his throat abruptly. "It will—but I've got to get him out first," he said bleakly. "You said five minutes."

They were working together and still grumbling as Thane left them, two men who had learned to accept the realities of their jobs and skim away surface emotions because that way you slept better at night.

Outside, the sun was warming the air. But near the front of the house stood a figure who looked very unhappy. Detective Constable Beech had arrived and was waiting alone, as if he'd been putting off coming to look for Thane.

"You heard what happened?" asked Thane without preliminaries.

Tight-lipped, his young face a study of dejection, Beech nodded.

"You were tailing him home." Thane waited.

"The report's on your desk, sir," said Beech. "I picked him up after he left Peebles's place and stayed with him. He didn't take the direct way home, just drove around for a spell without stopping. Then he came back here at 11:45 P.M., drove the car into the garage, and I—well, I waited down the road for a few minutes, just to make sure. Then I packed it in." He gestured awkwardly. "I thought—"

"Never mind," said Thane curtly. Then he gave Beech a

humourless smile. "There's no blame being hawked around by anyone. Not yet, anyway." He paused. "You saw him drive into the garage?"

Beech hesitated, his usual cockiness still totally absent. "He drove round to the rear of the house, sir. When I went past, I saw his car lights again for a moment—it looked like he was reversing in."

"He did." Thane thought of Doc Williams's preliminary estimate that time of death had probably been around midnight. It all tied in, the chance that Ellison had gone under the car to check the exhaust repair could still be totally plausible. "When you were tailing him, did you ever get close enough to hear the car's exhaust note?"

"You mean if it was noisy?" Beech shook his head. "No. But—well, you heard him drive away from Peebles's place, sir. How was it then?"

"Normal," said Thane.

Beech moistened his lips, as if going to add something. Then he stopped, frowned, and looked beyond Thane, down towards the road.

"There's someone else you could ask, sir," he said quietly.

Thane turned. A white Jaguar had just drawn in at the kerb and John Peebles was getting out of it. The Eurobreak managing director spoke briefly to the uniformed man at the driveway entrance, then saw Thane and said something more to the constable. The constable nodded and let Peebles pass.

"Thane—hold on." Face a tight mask, Peebles came up the driveway at a near trot. The man's white hair was ruffled, he looked as though he hadn't taken time to shave, and when he arrived he gave an agitated gesture towards the house. "How's his wife? She phoned and told me—and she sounded pretty bad."

"I've left her alone, Mr. Peebles." Thane glanced at Beech, who took his cue and moved away. "But she told one of our men Ellison went to see you last night."

"He did, for an hour or so—a business discussion. He left me around eleven." Peebles drew a hand through his hair, the platinum identity bracelet on his wrist catching the sunlight. "But in heaven's name, man, what happened here?"

"Didn't his wife tell you?" Thane found his cigarettes, put one between his lips, but left it unlit.

"Kathy?" Peebles drew a deep breath. "She babbled something about an accident in their garage and that she found him dead this morning. But—"

"It looks like he was trying to check a repair he'd made to the car exhaust." Thane put no expression into his voice and watched Peebles as he spoke. "The garage doors were closed and he had the engine running."

"The damned young fool." Slowly, Peebles shook his head. "It's a waste, Thane—a sheer waste. He had a lot of life ahead of him." He chewed his lip. "Another year or so, and I was going to have offered him a share in the firm."

"People can do fool things," said Thane. "Maybe his mind was still too much on the business he came to see you about."

"That?" Peebles shrugged. "I wouldn't say it was so desperately important, even though it had been worrying him. We've organised a new holiday package, two weeks in Greece at bargain rates. Ellison thought the profit margin was low, suicidal—" he caught himself on the word. "Now wait, that's not any kind of suggestion, Thane. I mean, there can't be any doubt about this being an accident, can there?"

"None I know about." Thane fed a shade of surprise into his voice and was sure that his words brought a slight, guarded relaxation in Peebles's manner.

"I didn't think anything else," said Peebles. He pursed his lips. "I'm not here just as his boss. We were distantly related—and that sort of thing matters to me. Now, particularly, when his wife is going to need help."

"I met her last night," said Thane. "I came round to get his help in tidying a detail about the plane crash."

"Yes, he mentioned that." Peebles shook his head slowly. "First Francis and that girl, now this—one damned tragedy after another, and you're left wondering what else can happen." He sighed. "I suppose it's just about as bad for you. Haven't you got that business about the aircraft sorted out yet?"

"No." Thane took the unlit cigarette from his mouth and tossed it away. "It still doesn't make sense."

"You could be chasing your tails over some mindless crank," said Peebles.

"Anything's possible." Thane let Peebles nod good-bye, then stopped him as he turned to go. "About that meeting you had last night. Was anyone else at it?"

"No." Peebles swung round quickly, his face blanked of expression, the lie coming smoothly. "Why?"

"In case he'd given anyone a lift home afterwards," said Thane, and twisted a faint, disappointed grimace. "It always makes life easier if we've a witness. If someone had heard him complain about the exhaust system—there's got to be the usual Fatal Accident Inquiry hearing."

"He said something about the exhaust to me." Peebles frowned, then shook his head. "A mention, that was all. Sorry."

Thane watched him go towards the house. Then he looked round, saw Beech still waiting, and beckoned him back.

"Get over to Millside," he ordered. "Tell Inspector Moss to contact Sergeant Gordon at Glenfinn. I want Gordon to find out when that Eaglefarm Crafts pair and their BMW got back last night—but I want it done quietly."

"Or he gets his hide staked out on one of his mountains?" Beech grinned with some of his old self-confidence. "Where will you be, sir?"

"At Headquarters, if I'm needed." Thane felt a slight chill at the thought. "There's an assistant chief constable waiting who may want my hide—but don't feel too happy about that, Beech. If it happens, there could be room beside me."

Chastened, Beech nodded and faded off towards the cars.

A good night's sleep had considerably improved Assistant Chief Constable Ilford's health. But his temper was another matter, and he made that clear within ten seconds of Thane arriving in his office.

"You're watching a man and he ends up dead—dead in a way that has a stink around it. Where does that leave us if the story ever gets dragged out in court?" Ilford leaned forward, both elbows on his desk, and glowered at the thought. "Thane have you any idea the kind of headlines a story like that could make?"

"Nice, big, black ones," agreed Thane. He was standing on the other side of the desk, hadn't been offered a chair, and it didn't seem likely he was going to be. "Except—"

"Except what?" Ilford cut him short with a growl. "Ellison lied, Peebles lied, you think these damned crafts shop people lied—and what kind of reasons can you offer?"

He snorted. "The chance this man Cassill was murdered, an equal chance Ellison was murdered—do you think that makes everything fresh and sweet?"

Thane said nothing. The sunlight coming in the window was hitting him between the eyes, but Ilford had positioned the desk in his new office with that in mind.

"It all comes back to that damned plane crash. Most of it, anyway." Ilford sank back in his chair, scowled down at his navel for what seemed an interminable silence, then at last looked up again. His expression was still granite-hard but his voice was more reasonable. "When are you going to talk to Ellison's wife?"

"This afternoon."

"Give her time to get used to being a widow." Ilford nodded a bleak approval. "Right, and I'll arrange a round-the-clock surveillance on Peebles—but we'll play the other half of it your way for a little longer, no direct pressure." His stubby fingers beat a brief, thoughtful tattoo on the desk. "What about the Glenfinn end?"

"I'm depending on the local sergeant," answered Thane. The loose ceiling tile above Ilford's head gave him something to keep his eyes on as he added, "His name is Sergeant Gordon, and he's a pretty good cop—though it looks like we're losing him."

"Why?" Ilford's eyebrows formed twin question marks. "What's his special moan?"

"Promotion and a transfer—he makes it sound like being sent to Siberia. To him, it probably is." Thane heard Ilford's grunt, but went on. "I said I might be able to talk to someone about it."

"In the middle of all this?" Ilford swore under his breath, but pencilled Gordon's name on his desk pad. Then abruptly, he changed direction again. "You saw the character who set fire to that plane at the airport. Could it have been Ellison or Peebles?"

"No, wrong build, sir."

"The Eaglefarm people?"

Thane hesitated, then shook his head again. All that left, he knew, was hired help. But in a city like Glasgow it was never hard to find, provided you had the right contacts and money.

"Well, it helps to know," said Ilford acidly. He shoved back his chair and got to his feet. "I'm now going to the Chief Constable's morning conference. All I've got to do there is explain this little lot to him." His mouth twisted at the thought. "That should be a happy interlude, believe me."

The main lobby at Headquarters was busy. It was the hour when divisional men were most likely to come in and when Headquarters staff decided they should disappear for a coffee break.

Colin Thane was threading his way through the bustle towards the main door when he heard his name called. A moment later, a small, white-coated figure reached him and gave him the kind of smile usually reserved for naughty schoolboys. It was the Chinese girl from the Forensic Laboratory and she had a twinkle in her bright almond eyes.

"Chief Inspector, you have been making my life very difficult," she said. "Either that, or I have a boss with a very odd sense of humour."

"If you're talking about Matt Amos, you're probably right," agreed Thane dryly, jerked out of the gloomy mood that had been with him since he'd left Buddha Ilford. "What have I done?"

"You sent me a very dead fish and a bottle of water,

right?" She stuck her hands in her coat pockets, pursing her lips in a pretence at anger. "Or at least, Matt Amos passed them on to me."

"Guilty," admitted Thane. "I was doing someone a favour."

"It was no favour to me." She wrinkled her small, turned-up nose. "Do you know the kind of chemical analysis your 'favour' got me involved in?" There was no chance to answer. "To simply say the fish probably died because the water was polluted—"

"Sorry." Thane grinned down at her. "Look, don't worry too much about it—there's no rush involved."

"And that comes rather late, Chief Inspector." This time the indignation was real. "You'll get my full report later—when I saw you, I thought you'd want to know the answer now."

"Yes, I do," said Thane defensively. "I know a sergeant who's waiting to hear."

"Well"—she paused for a moment as a group of typists flowed around them chattering and laughing as they headed for the canteen floor—"tell him it was nitric acid. Well diluted, but still enough to kill off any fish it met." She frowned and cocked her head, birdlike, to one side. "What I can't understand is how nitric acid got there."

"Some farmer got careless?" suggested Thane.

"A very strange farmer," she said. "It's a commercial acid, Chief Inspector. People use it to make things like explosives, dyes, celluloid, photographic film—or even in engraving. But not for growing things."

"You're sure?" Thane saw the warlike glitter coming into her eyes and hastily corrected himself. "What I mean is, you're talking about some kind of industrial process?"

She nodded. "If this Glenfinn place was near a city, I'd look for a factory criminally careless about waste chemical disposal. But in the Highlands—well, it's more difficult."

"Maybe not," said Thane slowly, his mind back on the Eaglefarm Crafts workshops. "I can check on it."

"Good." She smiled and turned to go. "Tell your sergeant I'm sorry about his fish—but a day or two should have everything else back to normal."

Thane's thoughts weren't on fish during the drive back to Millside Division. When he got to his office, Phil Moss was there and that meant spending the next several minutes telling him the Ellison story. At the finish, Moss looked as unhappy as Thane felt.

"I don't buy it," said Moss.

"That makes two of us." Thane glared at the age-scarred desk top. "Any word from Glenfinn?"

"Not yet. I got hold of Sergeant Gordon and persuaded him we meant it. He's checking. If anyone saw that BMW when it was heading back to the Eaglefarm place they should remember—he says it's the only one in the glen."

"Anything else?"

"No." Moss shook his head morosely. "How's Mary?"

"On her feet when I left." Thane got up and walked over to the window. The sky had clouded over in a way that could mean rain. His thoughts were on another woman, Ellison's dark-haired young widow, and the horror-filled way in which her morning had begun. "Phil, we had him scared—but not scared enough to take his own life."

"I'll go along with that." Moss came over to join him. "Why don't we really lean on Peebles? I mean all the way. There's plenty to work on—"

"We still need more," said Thane grimly. "We'll pressure him, Phil. But at the right time, and we're not there yet, believe me."

Moss shrugged. He was usually the one who urged caution and a slower pace. But the sheer frustration of their situation was getting through to him. His ulcer twinged, and a corner of his mind wondered if his normal judgement had been edged off balance by his own need for a personal decision.

There was a tap on the door. It opened, and Sergeant MacLeod came in ponderously from the main C.I.D. room.

"The overnight reports, sir," he said, laying a thin bundle of papers on Thane's desk. "The usual—you know about most of them."

Thane came back from the window. The routine side of the division went ticking on, regardless of crisis situations, and the overnight reports were part of it. With MacLeod waiting silently, heavy face a placid blank, he flicked through the pages and initialled some or put a query against others where he felt a follow-up might be useful. Then, suddenly, turning another page, he stopped, frowned, and glanced up at MacLeod.

"This leather-store robbery, Mac."

"Sir?" MacLeod looked surprised. "No problems. A traffic patrol car stopped this old van half an hour after the job. The stolen property was in the van, and there was only the driver aboard. The shop manager identifies him, he's got a record as long as—"

"Forget his record," said Thane, cutting him short. "What about his name?" He glanced at Moss. "Willie Kelly, from Fortrose—does that ring any kind of bell?"

"Hold on," said Moss slowly. "Yes, he's Soldier Kelly's cousin. What was he trying to get away with this time?"

"Travel bags, suitcases, hand luggage." Thane ran a finger down the typewritten list. "Enough to stock a shop of his own." He stayed staring down at the list, but no longer seeing it. His mind was grappling with a possibility that was incredible, almost ridiculous, yet impossible to ignore.

"Well, they'll be company for each other, sir," said MacLeod, not certain what was going on.

"That's maybe the least of it." Thane drew a deep breath that was in part a silent prayer. "When we picked up Soldier Kelly at the Fortrose code twenty-three he had a passport application form on him. Phil—"

"Uh?" Moss raised a puzzled eyebrow.

"Try the Passport Office. Ask how many applications they've had for passports from addresses in Fortrose during the last couple of days." He saw Moss's continued bewilderment. "Just do it, Phil. Now."

Moss nodded and hurried out, giving a shrug in MacLeod's direction.

"Sir—" began MacLeod, wishing he'd sent someone else in with the overnight sheets.

"Later, Mac," said Thane. He opened a drawer of his desk, brought out the Eurobreak brochure he'd been given by Ellison, and turned the pages till he located the section that mattered. Then he looked up at MacLeod again. "How'd you like to book yourself a holiday abroad—leaving tomorrow?"

"Me?" MacLeod's mouth fell open. "But I haven't any leave due and anyway—"

"I said book it, not go," said Thane. He tossed the overnight reports back across the desk. "Here, get rid of these. Then stay handy—and if anyone in this damned division has a lucky rabbit's foot tell him to start rubbing it."

MacLeod swallowed, nodded, and went out. Left alone, Thane read the brochure section again. Just as they'd been told on that very first visit, Eurobreak took care of all a traveller's needs—down to currency exchange.

He chewed his lip hard for a moment, thinking it through again. A dead fish, Soldier Kelly wanting a passport, his cousin stealing a load of travel luggage—added to the rest that they had, it made only one kind of sense.

Picking up the telephone, he raised the divisional switchboard and waited while they put a call through to the police office at Glenfinn. The distant number began ringing and kept ringing for what seemed an interminable time before the other receiver was lifted.

"Police, Glenfinn," said Sergeant Gordon, his voice breathless.

"Thane in Glasgow, Sergeant." Thane crossed his fingers. "One question, and I need a quick answer."

"If it's about the Eaglefarm folk, sir, I'm just back," answered Gordon over the crackling line. "I heard the phone going as I got out of the car."

"No, it's about that damned fish you sent," said Thane.

"Sir, I—" Gordon gave a groan "—och, I'm sorry about that. My wife gave me hell when I told her—"

Thane grinned at the mouthpiece. "Here's the question. How far away from the Eaglefarm place was the pool where these fish were dying?"

"Fairly close—a few hundred yards maybe." Gordon sounded bewildered.

"There was nitric acid in the water," said Thane. "Suppose it came from Eaglefarm. How would it get to the pool?"

There was a pause, when all he could hear was Gordon's heavy breathing and the continued crackle of the line.

"There's a wee trickle of a burn from Eaglefarm to the main stream, sir. It joins just above the pool." Gordon hesitated. "They've mainly septic tanks at that end of the glen. If I'd a dose of chemicals to get rid of, I wouldn't risk damaging the tank—yes, I'd either dump it in the burn or pour it straight into the stream."

"Right," said Thane with considerable relief. "Now how about their car?"

"That's what I was coming back to call you about." Gordon sounded as if he felt he was dealing with a madman. "I was lucky. Our local doctor was out overnight—delivered a baby to a farmer's wife down the glen. Her third boy, and—"

"The car," said Thane impatiently.

"He saw the BMW on his way back home, sir. The only other thing he passed on the road. That was at 3 A.M., so if they drove straight up here they couldn't have left Glasgow till after midnight."

"Thanks, Sergeant. It's about time we got lucky," said Thane. "I'll be in touch."

He hung up, lit a cigarette, and strode out into the main office. Moss was still talking on a telephone. But as Thane came towards him he winked and raised one scrawny hand in a thumbs-up sign.

That was the moment Thane knew he had to be right.

CHAPTER SIX

Phil Moss refused to be hurried. He spoke for a couple of minutes more, scribbling notes as his questions were answered, then cheerfully thanked the voice at the other end of the line and hung up. Sitting back, he grinned up at Thane.

"Passport Office say they've had four applications for first-time passports from Fortrose in the last two days. All male, and one of them is Willie Kelly. Recognise the others?"

Thane took the list Moss offered, glanced down the scribbled names and addresses, and nodded. Every one of the men was a ned with a record, a small-time layabout who had been handled by Millside Division times without number.

"Four," mused Moss. "And Soldier Kelly had his application form—which makes five." He considered Thane. "All right, it makes you some kind of a genius. But what the hell's going on? How does it tie in?"

"Luck," said Thane. He sat on the edge of Moss's desk, let the cigarette dangle between his lips, and looked around the drab C.I.D. duty room while one part of his mind tried to assemble the pieces again and another part still marvelled at the way a sheer hunch had paid off. "Luck and a dead fish."

"Eh?" Moss's eyes widened in surprise. "Look, you don't

mean that stinking relic you brought back from—" He didn't even bother to finish.

"Right." Thane took a last draw on the cigarette, dropped it on the burn-scarred linoleum, and ground it out underfoot. He reckoned he wasn't due another smoke before evening. "Or that's what started it."

"You wouldn't like to lie down somewhere?" asked Moss acidly.

"Shut up and listen," suggested Thane. Spreading his strong fingers wide, he gripped his knees and rocked gently for a moment. "The Forensic squad decided the fish died from nitric acid poisoning. The nitric acid got into that stream very near to the Eaglefarm Crafts place. Any idea what nitric acid is used for, Phil?"

"Surprise me."

"Among other things, engraving." He saw Moss's expression change radically and nodded agreement. "Fine-quality printing plates. So a craft colony like Eaglefarm, where there's an ex-printer like Harkness, might do some engraving work. But—"

"The plane crash when Manny Francis is coming back from there, the way it was searched and burned out—" Moss drew a deep breath. "Hell, and if you add this squad from Fortrose queueing for passports for a holiday trip—"

A telephone began ringing at the next desk. They both ignored it, and a young police cadet hurried over from the other side of the room to take the call.

"Keep adding, Phil," said Thane, his brown eyes suddenly sober. "Ben Cassill falls out of a window. Cassill is in the paper and stationery trade. Ellison ends up killed under his car. Ellison and Francis dealt with Cassill—and we'd scared Ellison. Maybe scared him more than we realised, till some other people became worried he'd talk."

"You mean Peebles." Moss moistened his lips. "Yes, but—"

"But Eurobreak Vacations sell holidays?" Thane nodded. "Right, except they sell a complete service. You can buy your foreign currency from them—pesetas, francs, marks, dollars, whatever. Currency you're going to spend abroad. Thousands of little happy holiday makers, buying their cheap booze and fags and souvenirs."

"All with counterfeit notes?" Moss picked up his ball-point pen again, and began a random doodling on the pad of scrap paper in front of him. "It would be a sweet racket. A horde of tourists—"

"Innocent tourists, who bought the fakes thinking they were genuine and paid regular exchange rates," emphasised Thane.

Moss grunted at the interruption. "There's been no Interpol feedback about forged notes. With the kind of operation you're talking about, I'd have expected people to be jumping up and down about it."

"Low-denomination paper money?" Thane shook his head. "We're not talking about amateurs."

"Strictly pro." Moss belched, a sign of aroused emotions. "Pro and prepared to kill. All right, I go along with it—and it answers the Inland Revenue mob's headache about Eurobreak's profits. If"—he paused then nodded—"if you add some clever crooked bookkeeping in the background."

"Some of the currency they sell could be genuine." Thane had been puzzling ahead on that one. "In fact, it would need to be if they wanted to put a gloss on things."

"Memo to Sergeant Gordon, Glenfinn," said Moss, getting to his feet. "That was one bloody wonderful dead fish." He took a deep breath, swelling his scrawny chest.

"So we know where we're going. But what's the next stage?"

"We stay clear of Peebles. Buddha Ilford has a tail on him and when his turn comes, I want to drop the world on him." Thane pointed across the room to where Sergeant MacLeod was making a laborious job of filling an expenses sheet. "We send Mac to a Eurobreak branch to book a holiday and order currency—and he wants to be on his way abroad before the weekend."

"Samples. How about our travel luggage raider, Willie Kelly? I could put him through the mangle about that Fortrose squad."

"No chance," said Thane realistically. All they had against Willie Kelly came down to assault and robbery, a twelve-month stretch which he'd hardly notice. But if he talked, Fortrose's hoodlum element would either leave him scarred for life—or he'd wake up dead some morning. "We want a Kelly. But we'll make it Soldier—and I'll do the leaning."

"Beech's notion, attempted murder?" Moss liked it. "Soldier went through court on remand this morning. That means they'll have shipped him on to Barlinnie."

Thane nodded. But that suited him too. The untried prisoners' wing at Barlinnie Prison was a place where most men had the edge taken from their confidence.

"I'll see him there. I want you for a digging job, into Ben Cassill's paper supply orders. Anything approaching bank note quality, Phil."

"Thanks," said Moss. The telephone at his elbow began ringing and he answered it curtly. Then his expression changed and he slipped a hand over the mouthpiece. "Surprise—it's John Peebles, looking for you."

Thane took the receiver and greeted Peebles in a carefully unperturbed voice.

"I want a favour from you, Thane," said Peebles. "I'm at my office, but I've just left Ellison's wife. Make sure your people go easy on her, will you? The girl is in the nearest thing to deep shock I've ever seen."

"We know that," said Thane flatly. "Have you any particular complaint?"

"No. But she's been told someone is coming back to talk to her. Damn it, she's had enough. Can't it wait?"

"Not for long," said Thane. "It's routine."

"In an accident case?" persisted Peebles.

"There's still a report to be made," said Thane. "Fatal accidents have their own paperwork."

"Well, I'm only trying to help the girl," said Peebles. "You'll make sure they take it easy with her?"

"I'll make sure," agreed Thane.

He hung up and twisted a humourless grin at Moss. "Peebles playing the good Samaritan. And fishing about how we felt."

"Nice of him," agreed Moss absently. He walked over to the city map which sprawled across the nearest wall and stood staring at it.

"Something wrong?" asked Thane.

"Your missing link." Moss peered closer at the map. "The character who burned out Francis's plane at the airport. I was thinking—" He stopped there, frowning.

"Well?"

Moss shrugged. "Just a notion. Let me check it out first." He turned and glanced at his watch. "I'll get Mac moving, then work on Cassill's paper orders. Where will you be?"

"On the move," said Thane. "Mrs. Ellison first, because of Peebles. Then Barlinnie and the city mortuary."

"I'll catch up with you," said Moss. He turned to the wall map again.

Thane left him to it. Back in his own room, he told the division switchboard he was going out then lifted the telephone again, called the city mortuary, and asked for Doc Williams. The police surgeon sounded mildly irate when he came on the line.

"Do you want me to answer calls or get on with my work?" he complained. "The average cop in this city seems to think he can have it both ways. If it's about Ellison, I've just started the autopsy—"

"And I won't hold you back, Doc," soothed Thane. "One question, and what matters is how soon you have an answer. If it was murder, but cause of death was still carbon monoxide poisoning—"

"How was he slid under the car?" Doc Williams finished it for him sourly. "I'm ahead of you." Then his manner changed. "You're really pushed?"

"Yes," admitted Thane. "He was part of a whole damned domino game."

"Then for you I'll skip lunch," said the police surgeon with an air of high martyrdom. "Make it 2 P.M. here and I might have something."

Thane thanked him and hung up. When he went out through the main C.I.D. room a moment later Moss had gone and Detective Sergeant MacLeod was getting ready to leave. But the other men around looked up as he passed and there was a different atmosphere in the air. The word was out, they knew things were happening.

It was 11 A.M. when the Millside duty car pulled in at the kerb beside Peter Ellison's home. The police cars which had been there earlier had gone, the garage behind the house had its doors closed again. As Colin Thane climbed out, leaving Constable Erickson on radio watch, he noticed a quick twitch of curtains in a bungalow opposite as an inquisitive neighbour peered out.

There was always at least one neighbour like that around. He went to the front door, where a now pathetic painted china plate said PETER AND KATHY ELLISON LIVE HERE and pressed the bell push. A young, red-haired policewoman, the girl he'd noticed on his first visit, opened the door and let him in.

"How is she?" asked Thane as the redhead closed the door again.

"Calmer now, sir." The girl nodded towards a room at the end of the small lobby. "She's in there, on her own. Some relatives are on their way from out of town, but I've been turning away anyone else, except for a couple of friends she wanted to see."

"Keep it that way," agreed Thane. "You'd better be with me for this. Have your notebook ready, but don't wave it under her nose."

"Like they told us at training school, sir?" asked the redhead with a frosty innocence.

Thane grinned, nodded, and let her lead the way into a large living room where the furniture was Scandinavian in style and the thick pile carpeting ran wall to wall. Kathy Ellison was in a chair near a broad spread of picture window. But her back was to the view, which was to the rear of the house and included the garage.

"Mrs. Ellison." Thane paused, then had to repeat her name again before she looked up at him.

Kathy Ellison's eyes were red and swollen and she hadn't done much more than run a comb through her dark hair.

She wore a matching skirt and sweater but her feet were still in house slippers. Her young face was dull and pale.

"I know you had to talk to police already," said Thane quietly. "But I've got to ask more questions—just a few." Out of the corner of his eye he saw the policewoman had her notebook ready. "Were you surprised when your husband went out last night?"

"Yes." Her voice was low and strained, then she showed a sudden surprised recognition. "You came here last night."

Thane nodded. "To ask his help about the plane crash. But he didn't mention going out."

"He had to see John Peebles," she said wearily.

"Couldn't it have waited till morning?"

"No. He—it was some business problem. He said there wouldn't be a chance to talk about it properly in the office. Things were—well, always too busy there."

"That happens," said Thane. "What kind of work did he do as an account executive?"

"Administration, planning, anything." She looked down, fingering her wedding ring.

"Did he get involved in the currency sales to customers?" asked Thane.

She nodded. "Partly—the branches ordered what they needed and he made the arrangements." Her eyes met his again, puzzled. "But—"

"So he'd be under a lot of pressure." Thane kept his voice sympathetic. "Plenty of worries. Or was that new?"

"It seemed to be getting worse. The last few weeks—" She stopped suddenly, moistening her lips. "You're not suggesting—"

"No, I'm not," said Thane firmly.

"You'd be wrong." Her voice trembled, the tears near

again. "The last thing he said to me last night was—was that the drive over would let him check the exhaust repair. He wanted to make sure it was right."

"He told us he didn't usually do his own repairs," said Thane. He saw the policewoman had edged closer and frowned her back again. "A noisy exhaust would get on anyone's nerves. Can you remember when it began?"

"About three weeks ago, I suppose," she answered listlessly. "I'm not sure. He was using my car most of the time."

"You mean he left his own car at home?"

She shook her head. "John Peebles borrowed it. His own car was in for repair for a spell and—well, he asked Peter for his. It was a firm's car anyway so I suppose Peter couldn't very well say no."

Thane turned away for a moment, startled, not wanting her to see his reaction. If Peebles had been using Ellison's car, then the reports linking a car with a noisy exhaust with Ben Cassill's death switched in significance. He made sure the policewoman was still writing, then turned back to the young widow.

"You heard your husband come back last night and put the car in the garage," he said slowly.

She nodded.

"What else can you remember, Mrs. Ellison?"

"I'm not sure." She gave a small, tight, choking noise. "I was only half awake. I—I think I heard the engine switch off. Then he started it up again."

"Right away or later?"

"I don't know." Her shoulders quivered and she brought her hands up to her face. "But if I hadn't gone back to sleep, if I'd only gone out—"

"You weren't to know, Mrs. Ellison," he said gently.

She was sobbing quietly and the red-haired policewoman was glaring at him. He looked down at the girl. There were other questions he wanted to ask, but they could wait another day. He laid his hand on her shoulder for a moment, then turned, shrugged at the policewoman, and left them.

Half an hour later Colin Thane watched a prison officer bring Soldier Kelly into the plain, bare interview room at Barlinnie Prison. Kelly came in with a nervous swagger, his eyes widened briefly when he saw Thane, then his expression changed to a forced, aggressive grin.

"Cops as visitors I can do without," he said thickly. "What the hell do you want?"

"Sit down," said Thane.

Shrugging, the thick-set ned straddled the hard-backed chair on the other side of the scrubbed wooden table. Thane sat back in his own chair and glanced at the prison officer, who nodded and left them, closing the door.

"Well?" demanded Kelly. "Keep it short, will you? The food here's rotten enough without me gettin' a cold lunch because of this."

"Complaining about the cuisine?" asked Thane. The old, grey prison, located on a low, windy hill on the east side of the city, was an overcrowded hell for men finding themselves in a cell for the first time. But for regulars like Kelly it was a case of familiarity making them feel at home. "I'll talk to the chef."

"Aye, do that," said Kelly uneasily, watching while Thane shoved back his chair and came round to stand over him. "Shouldn't there be two of you for a visit like this?"

"Call it informal, Soldier," said Thane. "You're going to have company soon enough. We picked up your cousin Willie overnight."

"Willie's thick as a plank." Kelly suddenly found the far

corner of the interview room interesting. "What did he try this time?"

"Grabbing a load of suitcases from a travel-goods store. Surprised?"

"Nothin' surprises me," answered Kelly.

"I'm different," said Thane. "I get surprises all the time. In fact, I like surprises. So how about telling me why a bunch of Fortrose's layabout scruff suddenly decide they all want passports so they can go abroad?"

"Any harm in a change o' scene? The cops here get monotonous."

Thane gave him a wisp of a smile. "So Willie grabs the luggage. Who pays for the trip, Soldier? Don't try to tell me you've been saving the welfare money."

"We got lucky with the horses," muttered Kelly.

"Horses." Thane considered him with disgust. "Want to try again?"

Kelly scowled and shrugged again.

"I've got my own theory," said Thane. "That plane crash, Soldier. Right?"

"Eh?" Kelly looked up at him with an attempt at outraged innocence. "Now wait, hold on—"

"Wrap it up," snapped Thane. With his right hand he grabbed Kelly by the shirt front and heaved him a full two inches out of his chair. "You looted that plane, Kelly. I want to know what you got and where it is."

White-faced, Kelly slumped back in the chair again as Thane released his grip. He moistened his lips, swallowed, and stared at Thane.

"Mister, you're stone, ravin' mad!" he declared.

"Soldier, right now you're charged with simple assault," said Thane. "Even with your record, that's maybe a ninety-day sentence. But suppose it was attempted murder?"

"Me?" Kelly's mouth fell open.

"Attempted murder," said Thane, his face impassive. "Trying to brain me with that hatchet. With enough police witnesses to form a queue. I'll guarantee you'd get twelve years—and it wouldn't be in any holiday camp."

"You know it wasn't that way." Kelly moistened his lips, leaving little blobs of spittle at the corners. "You're jokin', right?"

"Try me," invited Thane. He paused. "Unless—that plane, Soldier. The truth, and right now."

The ned sat for a moment like a man deflated, then, finally, he gave a small, weary nod.

"We nicked a parcel out o' the cockpit," he admitted. "It—hell, we were almost scared out o' our minds when we opened it." He swallowed hard. "Two million Spanish pesetas, so help me. Around fifteen thousan' pounds' worth—"

"New notes?" asked Thane.

Kelly shook his head. "Used."

"You're sure?" Thane hadn't expected that.

"I said so, didn't I?" Kelly was indignant. "All of it in five-hundred-peseta bills. We—hell, only the five o' us knew about it an' we were going to keep it that way. But the word got out an' that's what yesterday's war was about. Other people wantin' a cut."

"So where's the money now?" asked Thane. He saw Kelly hesitate, and warned grimly, "Attempted murder, Soldier—you'd be High Court fodder."

"I know." The ned swore sadly, then shrugged. "All right, but it stays at assault?"

"Assault, and we don't broadcast who tipped us," agreed Thane. "We'll talk about the theft charge after we get the money back."

Soldier Kelly winced but nodded.

"We did a three-way split," he said. "One lot's at my place, in behind the bath panel. The other two who have the stuff are Billy Garrison an' Doggy Spiers. I don't know about Billy, but Doggy Spiers has a window box."

"Thanks," said Thane dryly. "You wouldn't have liked Spain anyway."

"Why not?" he asked.

"The cops out there," said Thane, going over to the interview room door, opening it, and beckoning the waiting prison officer. "They're not friendly like we are."

Kelly glared at him, lost for words.

Even under Strathclyde, some things hadn't changed. Glasgow city mortuary was still the same low, red-brick block close to the banks of the river Clyde and usefully next to the Judiciary Courts building. Across the street, yellow daffodils in the flower beds at the entrance to Glasgow Green bloomed defiance at the surrounding grime of old tenement buildings and the stench from the oily river. And old tramp sat beside the flowers, a half-empty bottle of cheap wine in one hand as he watched the passing traffic.

At 2 P.M. exactly, as he'd arranged, Colin Thane arrived at the mortuary. An attendant greeted him just inside the main door.

"Heard the one about the terrorist wi' the hand-grenade, Chief Inspector?" he asked cheerfully.

"He couldn't count to ten," said Thane. "Where's Doc Williams?"

"Second sideroom along, havin' a mug of tea," said the attendant, hurt. Then, triumphantly, he evened the score. "No use askin' for some. There's none left."

Thane went along the tiled corridor, where the sideroom

door was lying open. He heard a murmur of voices then his nostrils caught the reek of a familiar pipe smoke which held its own warning. Entering, he found Ilford straddling a chair and sucking his pipe. Moss was perched on a radiator near the frosted glass window, and Doc Williams, who was in his shirt sleeves, used a filing cabinet as a table top for his tea mug while he munched a sandwich.

"All present, Doc," said Ilford. Then he gave Thane a nod. "How was Barlinnie?"

"It paid off, sir." Thane told his story, plus the visit to Ellison's widow, in a few tight sentences while Doc Williams looked interested but munched on. Moss's reaction was a slow, lopsided grin which kept growing till it threatened to split his thin face. Only Ilford stayed impassive, nodding occasionally, grunting with displeasure as his pipe gave out and leaning forward to knock the ash into a wastebin.

"So now we know," said Ilford unemotionally when Thane finished. He nodded wisely to himself for a moment then said it again. "Now we know. The less I hear about how you got Kelly to talk—" He shrugged and left it. "Well, I came here hoping. Doc, it's your turn."

"First hearing for all of us," complained Moss. "He wouldn't damned well start till you got here."

"Too right," agreed the police surgeon. He had finished the sandwich and swallowed a last gulp of tea. "Saves effort if I only have to tell it once."

Putting down the mug, he crossed to the small table in the middle of the room, picked up a clipboard, but didn't bother glancing at the papers in it.

"Post-mortem examination of the body of Peter Ellison, deceased." He paused, as if making sure he had his audience's full attention. "Do you want the lot, or what matters?"

"We'll rely on your judgement," said Ilford with a heavy sarcasm. "Get on with it."

"Fine." Doc Williams tossed aside the clipboard. "Straight off, death was due to carbon monoxide poisoning. No doubt of it, Colin—he had the lot. Congested lungs, post-mortem staining, bright red colouration of the blood, the usual petechial haemorrhages. Chemical tests of the blood were positive. Any arguments?"

Frowning, Thane shook his head.

"But"—Doc Williams brought his fingertips together then used them to touch his chin, making sure he still had their attention—"there's another matter. The exhaust has killed him, agreed. What's left is, how did it happen it killed him?"

"Like you're going to tell us now?" suggested Moss.

"Exactly," agreed Williams. "Modestly, I won't claim credit for all of it. Matt Amos took samples of dirt from Ellison's hands, the car exhaust and the garage floor then put them under a microscope. The stuff on Ellison's hands matched the garage floor—not the exhaust."

"So that part was faked?" Thane glanced at Ilford, who didn't comment.

"Next, why he just lay there and died—your question when you telephoned, Colin," said Williams, the last trace of humour vanishing. "That wasn't so easy."

"Even for you?" asked Ilford acidly.

"For anyone," Williams said. "But I can tell you what happened, and I'm not guessing. Someone slapped a pad of chloroform over his face first. He was unconscious when they fed him under that exhaust pipe."

Ilford frowned. "Spell it out."

"I will," nodded Williams. "Fact one, some tiny but totally significant abrasions around the nose and mouth. You need a magnifying glass to be sure, but they're there. Fact two, a rather unpleasant chemical test. It's a devil's-brew business involving body fluid—but it's a test sensitive enough to detect one part chloroform in six thousand." He paused. "The result was positive. That's how I'll report."

There was a long silence in the room when he finished, then at last Ilford stirred.

"Doc, suppose we got an exhumation order for Ben Cassill's body—"

"I'm ahead of you," said Williams. "I checked. His relatives had him cremated."

Ilford swore under his breath. "But it could have been the same thing there, a chloroform pad before he went out the window?"

The police surgeon shrugged. "I don't play guessing games, sorry."

"Damn you." Ilford reddened then subsided again. "No, you're right. Thane—"

"Sir?" Occupied with his own thoughts, Thane answered almost absently.

"I want to be quite sure," said Ilford. "What else have we got—guesswork or otherwise?"

Moss cleared his throat. "Nothing major"—he glanced at Thane, then went on—"but a couple of things could be useful. We had a man book a holiday through Eurobreak this morning and order foreign currency. He picks up the tickets and the money tomorrow—they couldn't do it quicker."

"Another day." Ilford nodded. "What else?"

"You need paper to print bank notes," said Moss dryly.

"Cassill was in the wholesale stationery game, with access to most grades of paper. His firm allowed him to operate a personal account for small private customers, ordering in his own name." He shrugged at the others. "With the kind of paper he was ordering, he could have started his own bank."

Ilford got up and prowled the sideroom for a moment, scowling.

"Fortrose," he said suddenly. "We start there, Thane. Get all the search warrants you need. The same goes for Eurobreak, Peebles, and this Eaglefarm place—for later. But I don't want any slip-ups, not now. You check with me anytime that anyone as much as coughs. Understand?"

Thane nodded. A moment later Ilford left them and as his footsteps receded down the corridor Doc Williams heaved a sigh of amused relief.

"Got this one right up his nose, hasn't he?" he said. "Uh —one thing I'd like to know. Who did you get to book this holiday and where's he going?"

"Sergeant MacLeod," said Thane.

"On a dirty weekend to Paris," added Moss. "But he doesn't get to go."

"Would he know what to do if he did?" asked Williams, and gave a bellow of laughter.

He was still laughing at the thought as Thane and Moss went out.

It was late afternoon when they raided Fortrose, which was good timing. School was out for the day, horse racing was over, so the bookie shops had closed, it was too early for the bingo sessions in town—that way, it was certain most people were home.

Six Millside Division cars took part, which meant eighteen men—twelve not counting the drivers, who had to stay by their vehicles to make sure they wouldn't be vandalised. At Soldier Kelly's apartment, his wife threw a pan of soup at a plainclothesman and cursed him when she missed. Turning over Doggy Spiers's place yielded a bonus, a small mountain of stolen cigarettes and a case of whisky that certainly hadn't fallen off any lorry. That left Billy Garrison's abode, where they had to kick the door in and an irate Alsation dog took a chunk out of a uniformed cop's ankle.

But it was worth it. Half an hour later, back at Millside, Colin Thane looked at the three plastic-wrapped bundles on his desk. Between them, they represented two million in counterfeit Spanish pesetas—in apparently used notes, as Soldier Kelly had said, but still counterfeit.

"Beauties," said the Fraud Squad expert from Headquarters, who had come over to contribute an opinion. "The best I've come across. I mean, look at them—the paper's almost right, the printing is good, ink colouration spot on." He rubbed five hundred pesetas between his fingers with an envious air. "Whoever made the plates really knows his job. I'd take a chance on passing this myself, anywhere."

"They're counted," said Moss. "Put it back." He poked one of the plastic bags, frowning. "How come they look used?"

"Easy enough." The Fraud Squad man grinned at his innocence. "You use a contraption like a domestic spin dryer —in fact, you can rig one from a spin dryer. Throw in some gravel and fine dirt, and what comes out looks like money that's been changing hands for years. Ever looked twice at a used note?"

"They're respectable," admitted Thane.

Even after the Fraud Squad visitor had gone, taking the

counterfeit notes with him, Colin Thane still sat staring at the spot where they'd lain on his desk. He stubbed his second cigarette in a row. It was only half smoked, but somehow it didn't taste particularly good.

"Mind if I wander off for a minute?" asked Moss.

Thane let him go. Ever since their visit to the mortuary, Moss had been disappearing for "a minute" at regular intervals. With Moss, that could mean anything from his ulcer to sheer cussedness.

But what did they do next? At Headquarters, an unusually reticent Buddha Ilford appeared undecided, opting out of any immediate decision. They knew John Peebles was at his desk in Eurobreak's head office—two plainclothesmen were outside, ready to follow when he left. A new report in from Sergeant Gordon at Glenfinn, who still had only a vague idea what was going on, said Eve Buchan and David Harkness were going through an apparently normal day at Eaglefarm Crafts.

He was reaching for the telephone, ready to kill some time of his own by calling home, when Moss came back in. For once, his second-in-command had an oddly penitent look on his thin, sharp-featured face.

"Colin, I think I'd better get round to telling you," said Moss, no humour in his voice. "I've a feeling I may have really fouled things up."

"You?" Thane showed his surprise. "How?"

"Being too damned clever," said Moss. He sighed, shook his head, and perched on the edge of Thane's desk. "Remember this morning, when I was looking at the city map in the main office?"

Thane nodded. "So?"

"It was this. The Ford used by the thug who set that plane on fire was stolen from the city centre, from a street meter bay. There was no garaging space nearby and parking anywhere around is as tight as a side-drum."

"With a traffic warden behind every lamp standard," agreed Thane. "But—"

"Take it my way," said Moss. He chewed his lip for a moment. "Our man couldn't go wandering around carrying a two-gallon can of kerosene while he tried to find a car he could steal. But suppose he brought the kerosene with him, in his own car—that he parked the first place he found a vacant meter, then went looking?"

"It makes sense," admitted Thane. "He picks the Ford, opens it up—"

"Brings the kerosene from his own car, loads it aboard and heads for the airport." Moss drew a deep breath. "That's how I'd do it. But that way, he'd have to leave his own car behind in the other meter bay. He dumped the stolen Ford near the airport, remember? Colin, there's no way he could have got back to his own transport before the meter time there ran out."

Thane understood now. "So he'd have a parking ticket—"

"Like you said, around there you find a traffic warden behind every lamp standard," said Moss. "I got the Traffic mob to list every parking ticket issued within a quarter mile of where the Ford was stolen." He saw Thane's expression and nodded. "That was the gamble, Colin. If he'd sense, he'd use a clean car as his start point."

"How many parking tickets?" asked Thane.

"Sixty-four." Moss twisted a grin. "Their best for the month."

Thane knew how it had gone from there without being told. The vehicle registration numbers from the parking tickets had to be fed to the Vehicle Index computer, which had its lair in the South of England. When the owners' names came back, the next stage was local—feeding them to the Criminal Records computer channel at Headquarters.

"Who did we get?" he asked.

"John Edward Semper. He owns a Datsun coupé, three years old. Two convictions for armed robbery, two more for serious assault."

Thane whistled and sat bolt upright. "Since when have you known?"

"All afternoon, since we left the mortuary. Look, don't think I was trying to score points. You had enough on your plate—I only wanted to check it out first."

"I'll forget you felt you even had to say that," said Thane. "All right, what's gone wrong?"

"Everything. The two men I sent to collect him tried where he lives first, then other places where he usually hangs out. But the word now is he turned up in a bar just after they'd left, got the tip he was wanted and"—Moss shrugged—"well, he was last seen galloping for the hills."

"Done anything about the car?"

"General alert to all mobiles," nodded Moss. "Report any sighting then maintain contact. But leave the rest to us."

"I wouldn't call it a disaster, Phil." Thane gave him a commiserating grin. "In fact, it's a damned good piece of work. Anyone watching where he lives?"

Moss nodded. "Just in case. I'd like a search warrant."

"Let's go take a look first." Thane got to his feet. "Search warrants take time—maybe we won't need one."

John Semper's home was a room and kitchen apartment three floors up in an old tenement building near Patrick Cross which clung to a faded respectability. The Millside duty car stopped a street away and from there Thane and

Moss walked round. As they reached the grim red sand-stone building a man in a shabby duffel coat came to meet them from a shop doorway. His name was Detective Constable Lincoln, he was the only Englishman in the Millside team, and every now and again he claimed he needed protection under the Race Relations Act. But for the moment all he looked was cold and bored.

"Nothing yet, sir," he reported.

"Right." Thane patted his jacket pockets and made a mildly surprised noise. "Phil, I left my cigarettes behind. You and Lincoln go and buy some."

Nodding solemnly, Moss led Lincoln away while Thane entered the tenement, climbed the worn stairs, and stopped at Semper's door. Scars on the door and doorpost showed evidence of past visitors, and the heavy main lock was rusted and broken. That left a simple cylinder lock a five-year-old could have opened.

There was no one on the landing. It needed only a moment and a plastic credit card from Thane's wallet to ease the lock back. He pushed the door open a few inches then waited until Moss and Lincoln arrived.

"Mice?" asked Moss, considering the opened door.

Thane shrugged. "Lincoln, what would you do?"

"Well, sir." Detective Constable Lincoln eyed him. "If there's a suspected break-in, I suppose we'd better take a look around."

"Two are enough," said Thane. "You stay here."

Lincoln showed his disappointment, but nodded.

Moss at his heels, Thane went in. The apartment had a sour, stale smell and the bed in the main room was a jumble of grimy blankets. The kitchen had old, empty food tins littered around and the chipped, dirty sink had its drain almost blocked by food scrapings. But the racing sheet lying on the table was that morning's issue.

"Let's get on with it," said Thane.

They set to work in a search operation which had all the fast yet unhurried precision that came from long experience. Working in the kitchen, Moss reached into the dark, dank recess under the kitchen sink, felt around the water pipes at the back, and brought out a cloth-wrapped bundle. Inside it were three clips for a .32 automatic.

There was no gun to match, but a framed chocolate-box portrait of the Queen hanging on the bedroom wall was too patriotic to be true. Thane took it down. An envelope was pinned to the back of the frame and inside it they found close on three hundred pounds in Bank of England five-pound notes.

"Well, he got paid." Moss held one of the notes up to the light and frowned at it suspiciously. "Looks genuine too—"

"Honour among thieves," agreed Thane. He glanced around the room and decided the job was done. "Tell Lincoln to file the report. Whoever broke in here made quite a mess."

"No consideration," said Moss. "None at all."

A first trace of dusk was creeping over the city as the duty car took them back to Millside Division. On the way, Thane radioed Command Control and heard the result going out on the main Command wave length a few seconds later.

The special search request to all mobiles to look for Semper's car was now backed by a description of John Semper along with the warning that Semper was probably carrying a gun.

There was a trace of rain in the air as they reached the Division office. Inside, a women's church guild were starting a guided tour but they dodged round that and escaped upstairs. The only two occupants of the C.I.D. duty room were Detective Constable Beech and a young police-cadet messenger.

"Couldn't be quieter, sir," reported Beech. He gestured at the empty desks. "Most of them are having a meal break."

Thane realised it was a long time since he'd last eaten. The cadet, who had been reading a comic book, was sent in search of coffee and sandwiches. Then, while Moss glanced at the last entries in the incident book, Thane went through to his own room and telephoned home.

"Sure you're not a tape-recorded message?" asked Mary when she answered the call. "Chief Inspector Thane is out, but sends kind regards—"

"Over and out," said Thane cheerfully. "I'm a live broadcast. How's your flu virus?"

"In retreat, but I think the kids are candidates now." She paused suspiciously. "All right, surprise me. You're going to be late?"

"Maybe overnight," he admitted. "I don't know."

"I said surprise me." Her voice softened. "Take care—I wouldn't like going to bed with a tape recording."

"Even in stereo?" he asked.

She laughed, said good-bye, and hung up. As he replaced his own receiver the cadet came in with a tray of coffee and sandwiches. Moss was close behind him and behind Moss, with no chance of warning, was Assistant Chief Constable Buddha Ilford.

"It's just a brief visit," said Ilford curtly. "I'm on my way home to eat, then I'll be back at Headquarters." He found a chair and dropped down in it, grunting. "So you still can't find Semper?"

"Not yet," admitted Thane.

"He'll turn up. That kind always do." Ilford scowled and

stuck his hands in the pockets of his overcoat. "At least we've got tabs on John Peebles again."

"Meaning we lost him?" asked Moss.

"For about an hour," said Ilford. "Late this afternoon— he left the Eurobreak place on foot at four-thirty, went into a department store, and the men tailing him lost him between floors." A deep sniff indicated Ilford's feelings about that. "Anyway, he walked back into the Eurobreak office later, carrying some shopping. It doesn't look as though he knew he was being watched."

"Let's hope that," said Thane. He started to reach for a sandwich then saw Ilford had more to say.

"Finding Semper stays a top-line priority," said Ilford grimly. "But not for you two. Your next job is at Glenfinn. I want this Eaglefarm Crafts outfit taken out of the reckoning—and I want it done tonight."

"It's a long drive," said Thane, glancing at his wrist-watch. "If we're going—"

"It's arranged," grunted Ilford. "The Chief Constable has borrowed a rescue helicopter from the Navy to take you up. Take-off time is 22.15 hours from Glasgow Airport —better tell your friends at Glenfinn to expect you." He got up and turned to go, then glanced back. "Any idea who broke into Semper's place?"

"No," said Thane. "I don't imagine we'll ever know."

"That's what I thought." Ilford's broad face creased oddly. Then he nodded and left.

Ten minutes later a phone call came in. The plain-clothes team working the area around Semper's home had located a back-street filling station where the man had bought a fuel can and had had it filled with two gallons of kerosene.

Half an hour after that, a patrolling beat cop in Marine

Division found Semper's car abandoned and empty in an alley near the docks.

John Peebles was at home. Neighbours called round to join him for drinks and were still there at 9 P.M.

At nine-thirty, Thane and Moss left for the airport. Each had a .38 Webley pistol in a hip holster, drawn from the Millside armoury. Scottish cops as dead, unarmed heroes had become an out-of-fashion idea any time it was known in advance that the opposition might start shooting.

CHAPTER SEVEN

It was a damp, dark night when the Westland helicopter beat its way up from Glasgow Airport. Above the noise of the rotors the pilot, a thin-faced, extrovert young lieutenant, shouted and pointed to some of the landmark features of the brightly lit after-dark city below. Then, as they rose through the cloud and the city disappeared, he offered Thane and Moss a stick of gum, began chewing some himself, and at the same time swung his machine north.

There was moonlight in plenty above the clouds, and it was like travelling above a sea of dull, lumpy white cotton. Still chewing gum, flying his charge with a lazy efficiency, the young navy man glanced round now and again to make sure his passengers were happy and grinned every time he saw Moss's tight, worried expression.

At last, he eased the Westland back down through the clouds, crossing his fingers and winking at Thane. The ground was a black mass below, but as the helicopter's lights flicked off and on in a signal an immediate, answering pool of light showed a little way ahead. Two minutes later they touched down on a patch of grass landing strip which was lit by the headlamps of three waiting cars.

"Thanks for the lift," said Thane as he and Moss clambered out.

"Any time," said their pilot cheerfully.

Moving clear, his two passengers felt the wind from the

whirling rotor blades and instinctively kept low. Then, as figures moved out to meet them from the cars, the Westland's rotors quickened and it took off again, climbing rapidly into the night. At the same time, the headlamps around were extinguished and the world became black once more.

"You're back again, sir," said Sergeant Gordon somewhat unnecessarily. The first to reach Thane, he frowned at the departing helicopter's lights and made a politely worried noise. "I'm still not sure what's going on—"

"You'll find out," Thane assured him, then glanced at the other men coming over. "Thanks for the reception committee."

"Secret agent stuff, Chief Inspector," said Gibby MacDonald, arriving next and grinning in the night. "We don't have landing lights on the strip, but we manage."

The tall, red-haired flying instructor was wearing his special constable's uniform. The other men behind him were similarly dressed. Including Sergeant Gordon, there were six in all.

"I thought you'd maybe want a wee bit of help," said Gordon cautiously.

"Your mountain rescue squad?" queried Thane.

Gordon nodded, and that brought a grunt from Phil Moss.

"Where's the dog with the brandy barrel?" he demanded.

The "specials" chuckled, but Sergeant Gordon wasn't amused. He made brief introductions, then turned to Thane again.

"Glasgow want you to contact them straight away, sir. I had a telephone call about fifteen minutes ago, a man at Headquarters—"

"Called Ilford?" Thane sighed as Gordon nodded. "He matters."

They boarded the cars and made the short journey along the landing strip to the flying club hut, which had lights showing at its windows.

"Any chance of a punch-up in this, Chief Inspector?" asked Gibby MacDonald, who had crammed in beside Thane and Gordon.

Thane shrugged, but Gordon, who was driving, glared round.

"In that uniform you don't ask questions, Gibby," he snapped. "You just damn well do what you're told."

MacDonald grinned at Thane.

"Yes, Andy," he said. "Sergeant, I mean."

Lorna Patterson was in the clubhouse office with a smile of welcome for them and hot coffee waiting.

"I like to know what's happening around my airstrip," she said, then glanced past him at Gibby MacDonald. "Particularly when friends get involved."

Then she signalled the others and they eased out, leaving Thane to use the telephone alone. In under a minute he had a call through to Headquarters in Glasgow and was connected to Buddha Ilford's phone.

"You're going to have to play this by ear," said Ilford curtly, without preliminaries. "John Peebles is on his way north, heading your way."

"Since when?" asked Thane, his grip tightening on the receiver. "I thought—"

"He was at home till half an hour ago," said Ilford. "Then he drove into town, left his Jaguar at an all-night car park, and picked up a self-drive hire car—a red Fiat coupé."

"Have we a tail on him?"

"No," said Ilford. "Too damned obvious on a late-night drive north. But I've passed the word. There's a patrol car waiting at every road junction that matters, and so far he's sticking to the Glenfinn road. In a hurry, too." Ilford paused, then added, "I checked the Fiat hire. He booked the car by phone this afternoon."

"Anyone with him?"

"No," answered Ilford. "If you're thinking of Semper, we still haven't a sniff of him."

Thane thought quickly. If Ilford was right, then John Peebles would be at Glenfinn inside another two hours. The hire-car arrangement had to mean he was worried, but the afternoon booking pointed to a calculated arrangement rather than a panic decision.

"You can raid the Eaglefarm Crafts place now or wait," said Ilford, as if reading his mind. "Too early or too late—take your pick."

"Thanks," said Thane wryly. Ilford was right. It was as big a gamble as flipping a coin. He drew a deep breath. "All right, sir. We'll be there, but we'll wait."

"Good luck," said Ilford and hung up.

Slowly, Thane replaced his receiver and went out into the clubroom where Moss and Sergeant Gordon's specials were drinking coffee.

"Luck is what we're going to need," said Moss when he told him, then belched in a way that brought admiring glances. "Two hours—that means this side of 1 A.M."

"You can stay here if you want," said Lorna Patterson, who had overheard him. Her grey eyes looked worried. "I was told not to ask. But what is happening, Chief Inspector?"

"That's the problem," said Thane. He signalled Sergeant

Gordon over. "How good are these specials of yours at staying low and keeping hidden?"

"By night?" Gordon gave a humorless grin. "Two of them are the best damned poachers in the glen."

"We're going to need them," said Thane. "Can you lay your hands on some binoculars?"

Gordon nodded. "Right here. We keep the mountain rescue gear in one of the hangars." He hesitated. "If we're still talking about Eaglefarm, how close in do you want to be?"

"As near as you can get us."

"They've a dog that runs loose at night." Gordon frowned, left them to talk to one of the waiting specials for a moment, then came back and nodded. "Lachie will cope with that."

"How?" asked Moss suspiciously.

Gordon exchanged a glance with Lorna Patterson. She chuckled.

"Lachie has a way with dogs," she said innocently. "Ask any gamekeeper around—he'd like to know the answer too."

They waited another twenty minutes at the clubhouse. The telephone rang once, with another message that the red Fiat was still heading their way, and Thane decided that was enough.

He ordered the others out to the cars. Lorna Patterson came with them, locking up the clubhouse as she left.

"Going home?" he asked.

She nodded. Gibby MacDonald was hovering a few feet away and Thane left them. When he glanced back, he saw her talking earnestly to MacDonald. The red-haired flying instructor laughed softly, kissed her, then hurried over to join Thane at the cars.

"Ready now?" asked Thane with a mild sarcasm.

MacDonald grinned. "You're wrong, Chief Inspector. She's mad as hell because I said she couldn't come along."

"They're the marrying kind," said Thane. He thumbed MacDonald towards the nearest car. "Let's go."

The little convoy of three vehicles bumped along the track to the road and set off into the night. Minutes later they dove through Glenfinn village, which was in almost total darkness. Most people in the glen had an early to bed, early to rise way of life. Another mile went by, then Sergeant Gordon, driving the lead car, switched to sidelights only. The others followed his example and the cars crawled along the road for another short distance, then turned off into a farm track, lurched onto a patch of level ground, and stopped.

"How far from here?" asked Moss as he got out and joined Thane, who was with Sergeant Gordon and Gibby MacDonald.

"As near as we're going to get," said Gordon. Then, as Moss sighed, he relented. "Five minutes, Inspector—no more. Eh, where's Willie?"

One of the specials came forward and nodded sadly as he was detailed to stay with the cars. Thane looked around the others in the faint moonlight which filtered through an edge in the clouds. They were grinning like oversized schoolboys, then he saw two of them were carrying shotguns.

"We're not going to fight a war," he said bleakly, conscious of the weight of the Webley at his hip.

"Then that's a funny sort of bulge you've got under your jacket, Chief Inspector," murmured Gibby MacDonald.

"Or is that the way they make hip flasks back in Glasgow?"

Thane sighed and gave in, but with a warning. "Nobody uses one of these things unless I say so—understood?"

They nodded, and he felt Moss nudge his side.

"Trust them?" asked Moss in a whisper.

"Just don't let them think you're a rabbit," said Thane softly. "They might blow your tail off."

Moss winced and looked more worried than ever.

When it came to night work, Sergeant Gordon knew his business. Leading the way through a stretch of rough scrub and a belt of trees, occasionally murmuring a warning as they reached a hazard, he took slightly less than his five minutes to reach the edge of a thin trickle of water which was the burn that flowed beside Eaglefarm. They followed it up a short distance then he stopped again and pointed. The farmhouse buildings were in clear sight ahead, with lights showing from the living quarters.

"Two men round the back, sir?" he asked quietly.

Thane nodded, and two of the specials slipped away into the night.

"The dog," reminded Moss.

"Lachie's department," said Gibby MacDonald.

Lachie had already gone, and they squatted down and waited while long minutes passed. Once, Thane thought he heard a muffled whimper but the rest was just the murmur of wind and the occasional hoot of an owl. Then a rustle of grass heralded the man's return. He grinned at them, gave a soft whistle, and the big mongrel dog Thane had seen before in the Eaglefarm Crafts yard padded out of the night and sat obediently at his feet.

"I told you," said Gordon bitterly. "It's a way he has."

Lachie was talking softly to the dog. He brought out a length of cord from his pocket, tied it as a leash to its collar, and secured it round a handy tree stump. The mongrel yawned, licked his face, and lay down.

"All right, what does he use?" demanded Moss. "Drugs?"

Gibby MacDonald chuckled, looked round to check Sergeant Gordon was out of earshot, and beckoned Moss closer.

"Lachie has a collie bitch at home," he murmured. "One sniff of her scent on his clothes, and there's not a damn dog in the glen wouldn't turn cartwheels if he wanted. Sex appeal, inspector—never fails."

They left the dog there and Lachie was despatched to watch the track leading from the road to the farmhouse. Gordon guiding, Gibby MacDonald close behind, the four men moved cautiously towards the lights ahead.

Three minutes later Colin Thane was crouching down behind the shelter of a low wall which overlooked the courtyard. Moss was beside him, Gibby MacDonald had a position near the one-time barn which was now the Eaglecraft showroom, and Sergeant Gordon was behind an outhouse to their left.

It was after midnight, but the same lights still blazed behind the farmhouse windows. Thane used the binoculars he'd brought from the airstrip, focussed on one upstairs window where the curtains hadn't been drawn, and was rewarded within a moment by a sight of David Harkness going past.

Harkness was fully dressed. He stopped briefly as he passed the window, stared out into the night, then moved away. Then, as if waiting was getting on someone's nerves, they heard music coming from a record-player only to be switched off again.

The minutes crept past. Then the next minor piece of excitement was when a door opened and Eve Buchan stood framed in the light. She wore trousers and a sweater and walked rapidly across the courtyard towards the outhouse where Gordon was hiding. Moss grunted in alarm then they both held their breath while she entered the outhouse and emerged again carrying an armful of logs.

"Keeping the welcome mat warm for him coming," said Moss with relief as the tall blonde went back into the farmhouse and the door closed. "If we'd had a bug on Peebles's line—"

He left it at that. They both knew the rest. Getting the kind of permissions needed for a wire-tapping operation was like being turned blindfold into a maze studded with legal land mines. Usually it only made sense in an operation that was going to last over a period of time—and even in blackmail cases the average Scottish court handled the results with distaste while defence lawyers screamed about invasion of privacy.

More time passed while the night cold seemed to seep into their bones. Occasionally, Thane shifted position as the Webley holster dug uncomfortably into his hip. The nearest to a moment of excitement was when Harkness appeared at the farmhouse door and called and whistled on his dog. The man waited then shrugged and gave up, closing the door again.

Then, with ten minutes to go before 1 A.M., they heard the soft pad of feet and a glimpse of a "special's" uniform, then Lachie arrived beside them, breathless.

"Car coming," he said quickly, and vanished again to tell the others.

Headlights lanced along the road a moment later and swung into the farmhouse drive. Thane tensed behind the low wall and brought his binoculars up as the little Fiat coupé came into the courtyard and lights and engine were switched off.

It was John Peebles, and as he climbed out the farmhouse door opened, Harkness and Eve Buchan both coming out to meet him. Through the glasses, Thane saw Peebles brush their greetings aside and lead the way straight back into the building.

As the door slammed, Moss flopped back down behind the wall again and gave a long sigh.

"Well?" he demanded. "What now?"

Thane chewed his lip. It had to have been a powerful reason that had brought Peebles north a scant twenty-four hours after he'd last met the Eaglefarm pair, with a long drive home still ahead of him if he planned to turn up at his desk in the morning as if it was just another day.

Ilford had said play it by ear. But Ilford was far away, maybe even in bed by now. It was the handful of men in hiding around Eaglefarm Crafts who mattered—and the decision to move in or wait was Thane's.

"There's an old saying," said Moss, giving him a crooked grin in the darkness. "When in doubt, do nowt."

He nodded a slow, reluctant agreement, then looked at the farmhouse again as a new light showed at a staircase window, then another appeared from an attic skylight. Something was certainly happening inside.

"Sir," the hoarse voice almost at his ear startled him. It was Sergeant Gordon, who had come wriggling over to join them. "When do we—"

"How the hell should I know?" snarled Thane in a whisper.

Gordon shot a glance at Moss, who motioned him away. The sergeant crawled back where he'd come, and had just reached the outhouse again when the main farmhouse door flew open.

Harkness came out first, followed by Peebles. Each man was carrying a wooden box, and they loaded them into the back of the Fiat, then stood talking for a moment before going back into the house. They left the door lying open and Eve Buchan came out next, carrying a smaller box which also went into the Fiat. The house door still lay open, the light streaming out, when she had gone back in. A new possibility came into Thane's mind, one which Moss put into words a moment later.

"It could be a close-down, Colin. Or a move."

Thane nodded, tempted by the open door not much more than a long stone's throw away.

"We could grab them now, with everything," urged Moss. "How about it?"

Peebles and Harkness were making another laden trip to the Fiat as he spoke. Thane drew a deep breath as they returned to the house, then nodded.

"Next time Peebles shows," he said softly. "Tell Gordon and young MacDonald—that's when we go in."

Satisfied, Moss crawled away. He wasn't long gone when a shape appeared again at the farmhouse door and started for the car. Thane half rose behind the wall then sank down again with a curse. It was Harkness, carrying a package which seemed as heavy as it was bulky. The thick-set craftsman had trouble getting the package into the Fiat and leaned against the car for a moment when the job was done, resting.

At last, hands in his pockets, the man went back indoors. Moss chose that moment to return and gave a silent nod. The others were ready.

Watching the doorway, Thane began counting slowly to himself as a way of keeping a brake on the tension he felt building again. Then he lost count, gave up, and a moment later scrambled to his feet, everything else forgotten, as the unmistakeable sound of a shot came from within the farmhouse.

It was followed by a muffled cry, the noise of something heavy falling over, then an angry shout. Thane sprang over the wall, starting for the farmhouse with Moss at his side, both of them drawing their .38s as they ran.

A loud smashing and clattering came from inside the glass-fronted showroom area, which was still in darkness. Then the whole window shattered outwards and a figure came catapulting through it, to land on hands and knees then scramble upright while stray shards of broken glass still tinkled down.

The man took three steps forward, saw Thane and the other figures rushing across the courtyard, and turned towards them. A second shot slammed out from the black interior of the showroom, and his arms flew up, clawing air for a brief instant before he crumpled and fell to the ground.

Still running, Thane fired two blind shots into the gaping hole in the window. He reached the fallen man, crouched down beside him as a bullet slammed one of the courtyard stones nearby and whined off in a ricochet, and was conscious of Moss kneeling nearby, triggering a deliberate, two-handed reply.

He rolled the man at his feet round and saw his face. It was David Harkness, and he was conscious, making faint, moaning sounds. Thane found he had blood on his hands, saw the spreading pool on the cobbles under Harkness, and started to rise again as Moss and the others closed in on the building. For the moment the shooting had stopped.

"No—please—" Harkness made a feeble grab at Thane's jacket. "Eve—she's upstairs."

"Peebles?" asked Thane.

Harkness managed to nod. "We—finished, he said. But we didn't think—this. When I went back in—" He couldn't go on.

Thane left him and ran over to the showroom. Moss and Gibby MacDonald had already gone in through the hole in the window and MacDonald had a torch out, playing the beam on overturned chaos which marked Harkness's blundering rush to escape. The Eaglefarm glass display lay shattered, and several shelves hung at drunken angles with their contents littered on the floor.

"Where's Gordon?" demanded Thane.

"He went in the front door with that mad basket Lachie," snarled Moss.

A distant shout, the snap of a pistol shot, then the flat, heavy boom of a shotgun stopped him there. They ran on through the showroom, emerged in the farmhouse's brightly lit hallway, and almost collided head-on with Sergeant Gordon.

"He got out the back way," reported Gordon breathlessly. "One o' the lads tried to stop him, but he's away—"

They followed him through to the back door, where another of Gordon's special constables stood scowling, shotgun cradled in his arms. Thane stared out at the night and the black silhouettes of the trees and knew their chances were slim.

"Try it, Phil," he ordered. "Don't let them stray too far." He shoved his Webley into Gordon's hands. "Go with him."

"Where's the woman?" demanded Moss.

"Harkness said upstairs. I'll check," said Thane. As Moss and Gordon started off, Gibby MacDonald went to follow them but he grabbed him. "Not you. Do what you can for Harkness, then call an ambulance."

MacDonald nodded and went in that direction. The stair to the upper floor was midway along the hall and Thane ran up the uncarpeted steps to the landing, then checked the rooms which led off. They were empty; then he remembered the light he'd seen from the loft and found another, smaller stair leading up to it.

At the top, he stopped short as his nostrils filled with the sickly sweet odour of chloroform. It came from a smashed bottle on the floor and a few feet away Eve Buchan lay motionless, a red patch of blood matting her blond hair. A table had been toppled nearby, and a considerable portion of the rest of the loft was filled with engraving equipment and a machine that looked like a small flat-bed printing press.

The heavy chloroform odour already gnawing at him, Thane dived towards the woman, grabbed her by the feet, and unceremoniously pulled her over to the stairway. From there he half-carried, half-dragged her down to the landing, then sat on the floor beside her for a minute with his head still swimming.

She was alive. The blood on her head was from a scalp wound, and she was breathing slowly and regularly. Forcing himself up again, Thane lifted her and carried her through to the nearest room where he left her on a bed. Going back to the landing, he took several deep breaths to fill his lungs then went into the loft again and used a heavy metal rule to smash the skylight window.

As the cool night air began coming in, dissipating the chloroform fumes, he reeled back to the stairway and returned to the landing.

Gibby MacDonald found him there, leaning against a doorpost, an unlit cigarette dangling from his lips, his rugged face still pale.

"What's wrong?" asked MacDonald, then stopped, sniffed the air, and understood.

"It's clearing," said Thane. "How about Harkness?"

"Dead," said MacDonald flatly. He looked past Thane and saw Eve Buchan lying on the bed. She was stirring, faint whimpering noises coming from her lips. "Do you—well, still want that ambulance?"

"For her?" Thane's mouth tightened. "Make it a doctor, Gibby. If she's fit, I want her talking first."

He went down to the farmhouse living room. There was a bottle of whisky on the table and he ignored the used glasses beside it, taking a gulp straight from the bottle.

That left him feeling better but still sick and bitter. He had gambled with Ellison, and Ellison had died. Now almost the same thing had happened again, and Harkness was dead.

No matter what the official reports might say, he was going to be left with that personal account—at least until they had John Peebles. Even then, he doubted if that would balance things out.

There wasn't much time to brood in the next hour. First, and to be expected, Moss and Sergeant Gordon returned with the news that Peebles had vanished, heading into the wooded hills. The special constables had gone down to bring their cars round to the farmhouse.

The village doctor arrived from Glenfinn, a sleepy-eyed man with iron-grey hair who refused to show surprise at the summons, his surroundings, or the condition of his patient.

By then, too, Thane had used the farmhouse telephone and knew that every road leading out of the Glenfinn area was being blocked.

If John Peebles was fool enough to try that way. Moss at his side, Thane walked out into the farmhouse courtyard and stared out at the faintly silhouetted hills which rose all around in the night darkness.

Beyond those hills lay a mountain wilderness, empty and desolate. Peebles was alone and on foot and a city man. But he was armed, dangerous, and intelligent enough to avoid the obvious.

The special constables had returned with their vehicles. One of them, a burly, fair-haired youngster, broke away from the others and came over, still nursing his shotgun.

"Chief Inspector—" He paused awkwardly. "I—hell, I'm sorry. I was watching that back door, but the way he came boiling out—"

"Forget it," said Thane. His eyes strayed to the shotgun, sensing the boy's feelings. But it was one thing to hunt and poach game in the Highland hills when it was as much a part of life as breathing—and another thing altogether when, for the first time, the target was a man. Any normal mind froze while the trigger finger hesitated. "There's a bottle in the house. Tell the others—call it a night duty ration."

The young special constable grinned sheepishly and went away, skirting round the spot where David Harkness's body still lay, covered by a blanket.

"I checked the Fiat," said Moss, his thin frame shivering a little as a low gust of wind murmured through the courtyard and stirred the trees beyond. "Everything's there—bits of printing gear, plates for half a dozen currencies, a numbering gadget, the lot." Turning up his collar, he scowled at the night. "Want to bet there's nothing left in that damned loft they couldn't cover with a legitimate excuse?"

"Close-down time," agreed Thane. For everything and everyone, as far as Peebles had been concerned. "We shouldn't have waited, Phil."

"So who gave you a crystal ball?" Moss belched rudely and nodded towards the men going into the farmhouse. "All right, suppose you had played it the other way. One of them might have ended up with a bullet in the guts. Would that have left you feeling better?"

It was close on 2:30 A.M. before the doctor from Glenfinn came back downstairs carrying his medical bag and agreed there was no reason why Eve Buchan shouldn't be questioned.

"Four stitches in a scalp wound and she's been sick a few times," he said with a yawn. "Your man had a pistol?"

Thane nodded.

"Then he most probably cracked her over the skull with the barrel, hard enough to knock her out. I'd blame the spilled chloroform for the rest—from what I've heard there wasn't time enough for it to be done deliberately."

That fitted with Thane's own thoughts, that the chloroform bottle had been dropped in the first struggle as Harkness tried to get away. He went along with Moss, and they saw the doctor out to his car, then once the man had gone they went straight to the upstairs bedroom, where Sergeant Gordon was standing guard by the door.

"My turn now, is it?" said Eve Buchan, in a harsh, sulky voice as they entered. She was sitting slumped on the edge of the bed, her raw-boned face still drained of colour, her mousy blond hair cut away at one side and the criss-cross pattern of stitches in her scalp clearly visible. "That hulk of a sergeant says you're expecting me to be grateful."

"Does he?" Thane pulled a chair over and sat facing her, leaving Moss to drape himself against the wall. "It doesn't interest me—not from you." He considered her grimly. "You know about Harkness?"

Briefly, something close to a flicker of pain crossed her face and she nodded.

"How close were you two?" asked Moss.

She looked at him and sneered. "What makes you think you'd understand?"

Thane intervened, nodded to Moss, and waited while he went through the inevitable formal caution. Eve Buchan shrugged as it finished, helped herself to a cigarette from a pack lying on the bed, and lit it.

"Well?" she asked, and waited.

"Let's save time," said Thane. "We know enough about the counterfeit money racket. But what happened to-night?"

Eve Buchan shrugged. "Peebles phoned this afternoon and said he was coming up. He reckoned we'd have to stop everything for a spell"—her mouth twisted bitterly—"or that's what he told us. He'd take the plates and anything else that mattered, keep them till it was safe again."

"Was it a surprise?" asked Moss.

"For Dave, yes." Mentioning Harkness's name made her look away. "I'd expected it, the way things were fouling up."

"So Peebles arrived," continued Thane. "Then what?"

"We talked. He said the tax men were sniffing around Eurobreak too much, that he was tripping over police every way he turned—that the only thing to do was sit tight, make the travel agencies a clean operation for a time, then pick when we'd start again." She took a long draw on the cigarette and let the smoke trickle out slowly. "We believed the swine. Even helped him load the gear into his car."

"We saw," said Thane. "Like we saw him shoot Harkness. What happened to you?"

"Dave went down to the car with the last load." She brooded for a moment. "That left me with Peebles. Then he had a gun in my back—and that's when he told me. There would be a fire and the locals would find two bodies afterwards. He said sorry"—her lips shaped a bitter, mirthless laugh—"but that's how it had to be. Then he must have hit me. That's all I know."

"Wrong," said Thane softly. "You know a lot more." He saw her eyes narrow but saved the next real question for a moment. "How did it begin?"

"Eaglefarm Crafts was a flop," she said wearily. "Dave and I were flat broke at the end of the first year. I knew Peebles from—well, way back. So I asked him for help, but he was in money trouble too. Then he came up with the idea that Dave could engrave counterfeit plates." She shrugged again. "We went along with it. Like Dave said, it wasn't as if it was British money."

"God save the Queen," said Moss. He glanced at Thane, drew a fractional nod, and eased off his wall, coming across to stand over her. "How about that bottle of chloroform in the loft?"

"What chloroform?" she said uneasily.

"The bottle you and Harkness got from him to kill Peter Ellison," suggested Moss. "Peebles wanted it back, didn't he? Except you didn't know why." He smiled at her. "Like me to tell you what you were wearing last night, or the time you left Peebles's place?"

She stared up at him, mute with surprise.

"So I'll tell you all we have to do," murmured Moss. "Maybe we find fingerprints on that bottle, maybe we don't. But we check your shoes, your clothes—Harkness's too. A smear of dirt or a few specks of grit from Ellison's garage floor—that's all we'll need, and we know a man named Amos who has a big microscope and can be very, very patient."

The cigarette had dropped from her fingers onto the carpet but she didn't seem to notice. Silently, Thane stood on it and ground it out.

"Suppose"—she stopped and moistened her lips—"suppose I told you I was there, but it was Dave who killed him?"

"Would you?" asked Thane quietly.

Eve Buchan looked down at her feet for a moment then shook her head.

"Dave and I—it was a special kind of thing we had going," she said. "But I had to do the leading. He was just made that way." Her head came up defiantly. "Anyway, what the hell? They call it life imprisionment, but you get out under ten years, right? I'll collect that much anyway on the money charges and they'd run—what's the word?"

"Concurrently, together," said Thane, knowing the odds were she was right. "Why was Ellison killed?"

"It was him or us." Talking suddenly didn't seem to matter any more to her. "Maybe he projected like the original bushy-tailed young genius, and he fixed the books for Peebles—fake currency purchase vouchers, all the rest. But he had no guts." A note of contempt entered her voice. "He'd lost his nerve, if he ever had any. So—yes, you're right. Once we'd decided, Peebles gave us the chloroform bottle and we were waiting at the garage when Ellison came home."

"Just like that." Moss shook his head with disgust.

"Don't think we enjoyed it," she said wearily. "Dave threw up once we got back in our car. He'd wanted Peebles to do it, but Peebles said no, that—"

"That it was your turn?" suggested Thane. "Because he'd been the one who eliminated Ben Cassill?"

"You've been busy, haven't you?" Eve Buchan considered them with a new and grudging respect. "Yes. Damn Cassill—and Manny Francis too. That's when things began to come apart at the edges. You know why, I suppose?"

"We can make a good guess," said Thane.

"Cassill was just a pal of Manny's who sold us paper. But Manny went drinking with him one night, had too much, said too much, and the next thing Cassill wanted in on the deal—a king-sized cut to keep his mouth shut."

"Blackmail," said Moss. "Nasty of him. How did Manny Francis feel about his pal being killed?"

"Peebles didn't tell him till afterwards. What we didn't expect was that he'd take it so badly, start hitting the bottle, and crash that damned plane."

Thane exchanged a satisfied glance with Moss. It was another, almost the final link in the chain.

"Where did Semper fit in?" he asked.

"Who?" She looked at them blankly.

Moss scowled. "Didn't you know Peebles had a tame thug on tap?"

"No, but I'd have been surprised if he hadn't," she said, then rested her head in her hands for a moment. "Look, I don't give a damn any more. But I'm feeling like—well, can't the rest wait?"

Thane saw the grey exhaustion on her face and nodded.

"Turn her over to Sergeant Gordon, Phil," he said. "Tell him a holding charge will do for now and to bed her down in a cell somewhere."

Moss beckoned and Eve Buchan rose. She reached the door, then glanced back.

"Want a laugh?" she asked in a flat, unemotional voice. "Any time in the last year Dave and I could have made it on our own, without the currency game. Eaglefarm Crafts had begun working out. We were doing fine on our own. Funny, isn't it?"

Moss took her out. A little later, Thane heard a car drive away.

Harkness was dead. Eve Buchan out of the reckoning. He lit a cigarette and went downstairs after a minute to stand at the farmhouse door. Harkness's body had been removed from the courtyard and more cars had arrived, the policemen who had come in them standing around talking and waiting. He saw Moss was with some of the special constables. They included Lachie, and the black mongrel dog that belonged to Eaglefarm was at the poacher's side.

"Here's what you need," said Gibby MacDonald, arriving at his elbow from the direction of the farmhouse kitchen. MacDonald pressed a steaming mug of coffee into his hands and added, "It's warm and wet—though that's all I'll guarantee."

Thane thanked him and stayed in the doorway, sipping the scalding liquid.

"Not much more than three hours and it'll be daylight," mused MacDonald, leaning beside him. He nodded out at the darkness. "With what's out there, this Peebles character could take a lot of finding."

"He's somewhere, and he can't hide forever," said Thane wryly. "We'll have more men by then."

"Those mountains could swallow an army." A frown crossed MacDonald's freckled face. "It can be hard enough in mountain rescue, when we go looking for someone missing, not hiding. But—well, ever heard of air search patterns? Low level search by light aircraft, Chief Inspector. We use it often enough and if you're lucky you save a hell of a lot of time."

Thane stared at him, the words registering but in a way suddenly and totally different from MacDonald's meaning. It was the one factor he had overlooked, one that might be critical.

"Peebles is a flier, Gibby."

It took a moment, then MacDonald's eyes widened.

"He could have doubled back," said Thane. "He knows he can't get out by road. But suppose he wants us to think he's trying to lose us in the mountains. Suppose he's really heading for the airstrip. How easy would it be to grab an aircraft?"

"One of ours?" MacDonald rubbed a hand along his chin. "They've ignition keys, like cars, but he could jump the wiring. Any pilot could handle a Piper Cherokee. The only other thing he'd have to do would be top up the tanks."

"If he did, how far could he get?" asked Thane urgently.

"A Cherokee's standard cruising range is four hundred miles," said MacDonald unhappily. "That could get him right out of the country."

"Would we know where?"

MacDonald shook his head. "Depends how good he is. If he wave-hopped and stayed lucky, even the defence radar boys might not spot him. But even so—" his voice died away doubtfully.

"What's his problem?" asked Thane impatiently.

"He's a stranger," said MacDonald. "He doesn't know the flight paths around here. If you're local or if it was someone like Manny Francis who came here often then a night take-off is reasonable enough. But if I was someone like Peebles, I wouldn't risk it."

"You're not on the run from a murder charge," snapped Thane.

"No." The young flying instructor bit his lip, took a couple of steps out into the open and seemed to be listening for a moment. "But—"

"We'll find out," said Thane, cutting him short. He drained the rest of the coffee, almost burning his throat, then shoved the empty mug into MacDonald's hands. "Get ready to go."

Then he hurried across the courtyard to tell Moss.

Two carloads of men left the farmhouse in a matter of moments, driving fast towards the landing strip. They passed through Glenfinn village as a rush of headlights and the only person who saw them was a startled local councillor, who was sneaking home after an exhausting visit to someone his wife didn't know about.

The road remained empty beyond the village, and minutes later the airstrip showed ahead. Swinging left, both cars bounced along the track that led to the flying-club hut and drew up with a squeal of tyres.

Thane and Gibby MacDonald sprinted to the clubhouse door. It lay broken open, and that was enough. Spinning round, Thane turned towards the hangars and as he began running again an aircraft engine coughed to life. It revved furiously, then the slim shape of a red Piper Cherokee began taxiing ahead of them, steering for the runway.

Cursing, Thane pounded towards it. Behind him, one of the police cars started up, made a skidding turn, and spat gravel and earth from its tyres as it charged in pursuit.

But the Cherokee had the edge on them. Rolling on, it reached the start of the runway, faced round smoothly on its tricycle undercarriage, and then bellowed up to full power. The faint red night-glow of its instrument lighting showed the silhouetted figure of John Peebles in the cockpit—then it started down the runway at a rush.

Outstripped by the police car, knowing even then the car hadn't a chance now, Thane came to a breathless halt. The Cherokee's wheels cleared the ground and the little aircraft began climbing, a droning shape heading rapidly into the night.

Panting up, Moss and Gibby MacDonald reached him and stopped. On ahead, the police car slowed and began coming back.

"Hell mend him," gasped Moss, his thin chest rising and falling rapidly. "He—he must have been sitting in the damned thing, all set to go."

Thane nodded and turned urgently to MacDonald.

"Gibby—"

The flying instructor didn't seem to hear him. He was staring into the night, all his attention still apparently fixed on the fading engine note.

"Gibby"—Thane grabbed his arm—"look, if we alert the radar defence mob—"

"Wait," said MacDonald quietly.

Something in his manner made them obey, while the police car coasted up and halted and other figures reached them out of the darkness.

It happened a fraction of a second later. All Thane heard was a sudden, distant thud, the Cherokee's engine-note change to a screaming howl, then a fluttering broken shape fell through a patch of pale moonlight. There was a second, softer thud followed by a sunburst eruption of flame.

After a moment, Thane realised he was still gripping MacDonald's arm. He let go, and MacDonald gave him a strange, sad smile.

"I tried to tell you back at the farmhouse," said Mac-Donald. "The wind meant a northwest take-off, up the glen. No problem if you know the flight path—except that six months ago the Hydro-Electric Board strung a set of power lines on damn great pylons across the head of the glen."

"He wouldn't know," said Moss, staring in fascinated horror at the distant, cherry-red flames.

"The only way to clear them is to gain height, all you can, fast," said MacDonald grimly. "We kicked up hell about the danger when they started it, but—" he stopped and shook his head. "Up here, it never pays to be a stranger."

It was about a mile to where the Cherokee had crashed, and the flickering flames acted like a beacon as the airstrip's emergency tender made a bumping, cross-country journey towards the scene.

When they arrived, the flames were beginning to die, and the broken, burning remains of the aircraft resembled the cremated shell of some hideously smashed insect.

The Cherokee had fallen slightly to the right of one of the tall pylons, into an area of thick heather and low scrub. Broken power cables and the heavy, ozonelike smell which laced the smoke-filled air told the rest and fragments of wreckage littered the ground for yards around.

Standing beside a mangled section of tailplane, watching the other men moving aimlessly around, Thane heard a sudden shout. Then, like the rest, he headed quickly to a spot on his left where a special constable was staring down at something dark and motionless on the ground.

"He's alive, sir," said the man in a sick voice, then turned away quickly.

How John Peebles had got out, how he'd dragged himself some fifty yards from the burning aircraft, Colin Thane couldn't even begin to imagine. But, waving the others back, fighting down the nausea he felt at the stink of charred flesh, he knelt close beside the horribly burned husk which still breathed and which looked up at him with eyes glazed by an agony of pain.

Only a few scorched fragments of clothing still clung to Peebles's tortured body. His left hand was like a flame-roasted claw, the platinum identity bracelet a blackened band against raw flesh.

"Thane." It came like a rasping whisper, Peebles's lips hardly moving. "Nearly made it, right?"

"Nearly," said Thane quietly.

"Power cables. Didn't know—about them." Peebles tried to stir and his whole body shivered in pain. He sank back but spoke again after a moment. "Well, you've got it neat and—and tidy now. No loose ends."

"Just one," Thane corrected him softly. "We haven't got Semper. Did you—?"

"Him? No." The scorched lips tried to twist a cynical smile. "He didn't know much and his—his kind don't talk. So I gave him a bundle of money—real money—and told him to get lost. Thane, he—he'll take some finding. He had a pal aboard a ship that was sailing last night." A long sigh followed, then the eyes almost closed but opened again.

"To hell with it," said what was left of John Peebles, and died.

It was midday before Thane and Moss could fly back to Glasgow, then Thane had to go straight from the airport to a Headquarters session with Assistant Chief Constable Ilford. That lasted until late in the afternoon, when he returned to Millside Division. It was raining hard when he got there and the windows in the C.I.D. duty room were running with condensation.

Phil Moss was waiting for him in Thane's office and looked as tired-eyed as Thane felt.

"How did it go with Ilford?" asked Moss as Thane slumped into his chair.

"He'd have liked it tidier," said Thane.

Though the only really loose end remained Semper. Maybe John Peebles had been right and the man had got aboard one of the many ships that had sailed from the Clyde. But it was pretty well inevitable that he'd turn up on a police report somewhere, sometime—and he was almost an incidental.

The rest came down to reducing a string of deaths to a series of reports and statements and all the rest of the mop-up operation, including the charges against Eve Buchan.

At least Sergeant Gordon wouldn't have to move. He'd wrung that promise out of Ilford. Sergeant Gordon could hang on at Glenfinn and get first chance at a step up in his own area.

"Uh, did Buddha say anything else?" asked Moss anxiously.

"Like what?"

"The Promotions Board," snarled Moss. "What else?"

Ilford's comments in that direction had been caustic but not final.

"He told me to get my hair cut," admitted Thane with a grin.

Moss sighed and headed for the door.

"Mary phoned," he said as he went out. "Better call her. The kids haven't got flu. It's measles."

Outside, Moss reached his own desk and scowled down at it for a moment, listening to the rain beating on the windows. Then he gave a low-key belch, lifted the telephone, dialled the City Mortuary, and asked for Doc Williams.

He sighed to himself as the police surgeon came on the line.

"Doc, no promises. But how'd you like to talk to a real, live patient for once?" he asked.

If everything else was changing, he might as well go along with the fashion.